First & Forever

the

crescent chronicles

ALYSSA ROSE IVY

Other Books by Alyssa Rose Ivy

www.AlyssaRoseIvy.com
www.facebook.com/AlyssaRoseIvy
twitter.com/AlyssaRoseIvy
AlyssaRoseIvy@gmail.com

First

a crescent chronicles novella

Chapter One

"Looks like tonight's activity just arrived." Jared's comment made me snap my head up from the bar. The only activities my friend cared about involved girls—he had my attention.

It didn't take long to see what caught his eye. She was gorgeous—especially those long tan legs that were shown off nicely in the short yellow dress she wore. Slim but clearly athletic, I could only imagine how much fun she'd be.

I finished off my Jack and Coke, slamming the empty glass down on the mahogany bar. The new guy who'd bought the place had gone to town on the hunk of wood. I doubted he had any idea that the hotel he'd purchased housed a hell of a lot more than rooms, food, and booze.

The girl walked around the lobby like she owned the place, her eyes taking in every detail. Finally they found me, and I got a look at her bright green eyes. I gave her my trademark smile. It worked every time. She smiled back, and I nodded, telling her to come over. I thought she was going to, until she shook her head and kept on walking. She didn't even give me a second glance. What the hell?

So focused on her retreating figure, I was barely aware of Jared talking. "I call dibs on the blonde."

"Blonde? She was a brunette." He must have been losing it.

My other friend, Owen, laughed. "There were two girls, Levi."

"Oh, I only noticed the one." Had there really been someone else with her?

Jared smirked. "You seriously didn't notice that blonde? That top didn't leave much to the imagination."

"Did you see where they went?" I really didn't care about the blonde, but I had to find Miss Legs. I couldn't believe she'd blown me off like that. Maybe I was right— she was going to be a lot of fun.

"They're probably in the courtyard." Owen yawned. He seriously worried me sometimes. A girl dumped him, and he'd practically been a monk since. The guy needed to get laid. Jared and I were going to have to try harder to get him out there.

"I could really use a night with that one." I turned to Owen. Our taste in women had always been more similar. Jared only went for busty blondes, where as I wanted the brunettes with the long legs. A nice chest didn't hurt—not at all, but a short skirt on the right girl could drive me crazy.

"I noticed her." Owen's small smile would have been enough for me to let him have her usually, but this one was for me.

"I've got to find her. She might even be worth a second night." Or a third.

Owen snorted. "Real nice."

I shrugged. "Just saying."

Jared finished his drink. "We'll find them, but we need to get moving. Your dad's going to get pissed if we're late."

"Yeah, I know." I left a twenty on the bar and took one last glance around to make sure she hadn't changed her mind and come back, before I walked over to the elevator. I smirked at the weird bellboy that was always staring at us. He took a step back and lowered his eyes.

Once the doors shut, I inserted the key card and pushed the button for the basement. The central offices and chambers of the Society were housed on a level of the hotel that wasn't supposed to exist. It was better for everyone if humans didn't go looking for us. When you're a prince of a supernatural society, you understand the importance of keeping some things secret.

"What do you think he wants us for this time?" Jared asked, leaning back against the wall.

"Like I'd know, but he didn't sound happy." I listened to one message, but it was only the latest of many. My dad's calls were always the same. Either I'd done something wrong, or I was about to do something wrong.

Jared stuffed his hands in the pockets of his jeans. "I guess we'll find out."

The elevator doors opened, depositing us into a room that would be dark for the average person, but we had no problem seeing. One of the benefits of being a Pteron was perfect night vision. I pushed open the doors, and we headed toward my dad's office, which was located just off the main chamber.

I knocked on the door loudly. "Who is it?" Dad called.

I knocked one last time just to be a pain. "Who do you think?"

"Come in, Levi." His low, gravelly voice always sounded pissed when he talked to me.

I walked in, Owen and Jared followed behind.

Dad didn't glance up from the paperwork on his desk. "Close the door."

Jared slammed the door harder than he needed to. The action wasn't lost on my dad. He finally dropped the paperwork, and his glare had Jared standing up straighter.

Dad didn't miss a beat. His steely gaze moved to me. "You missed last night's council meeting."

"What are you talking about? We just met last week."

"I called an emergency meeting last night." He ran a hand through his gray hair. At one time, it had been the same shade of brown as mine, but time, or too many years as the King of The Society, had aged him.

Shit. I should have listened to the other messages. "Yeah, well, I didn't know."

"Is that all you have to say for yourself? Twenty-two years old, and you behave like a child."

My dad never minced words, but he usually kept his cool. Things had to be serious for him to be flipping out on me in front of my friends.

"I'm sorry. It won't happen again."

"It better not." His icy stare left little doubt he was serious.

"What did you discuss?" I shifted uneasily from foot to foot. Only my father had the ability to make me nervous. Most people were afraid of me or kissed up to me to get what they wanted. There were only four exceptions. Owen, Jared, and my parents.

"The Blackwells. There's talk of a takeover attempt."

"Like those Yankees could do anything," Jared spat. He never kept his mouth shut, not even in front of my father.

"Has your father taught you nothing, Jared? The second you start underestimating your opponent, you've lost your advantage."

"Yes, sir." Mentioning Jared's father usually had that effect. His dad was essentially the head of security for my family. We'd spent many nights getting wasted and talking about how much we hated our fathers. Neither of us would ever live up to their expectations.

"So what's the plan?" I slunk down in a high back chair. This could take a while.

"The plan is that you grow up and find a girl."

"This again? I'm not ready. Just because you and Mom got married at twenty doesn't mean I have to do it." I looked for a mate once and all it brought me was heartache. What was the point of torturing myself again? I'd put it off as long as I could.

"You're not twenty. You graduate college in less than a year; it's time to stop chasing after everything in a skirt. Find someone worth your time."

"What does this have to do with the takeover attempt?"

"Don't play stupid." His cold blue eyes locked on mine.

"No one cares whether I have a mate. They know I can have a kid, it's not a big deal."

"Everyone cares. Everyone." He cracked his knuckles. He only did that when he was particularly worried.

"I'll take a mate when I meet the right girl." I leaned back in my chair and stretched out my legs. Getting angry wasn't going to help the situation, but I was tired of this bullshit.

"You can't find her unless you look."

"He does plenty of looking," Owen mumbled under his breath.

"Looking for a mate is different from looking for a girl to jump in bed with. I'd have thought you'd understand that, Owen." Dad really liked to get you where it hurt.

"You told me I have until graduation. That's months from now." I planned to enjoy every last day of my freedom until then, starting with tonight. I needed to get out of the meeting so I could find the girl.

"Building a relationship takes time. Do you expect to meet someone and bind yourself to her the next day? Don't wait too long."

Jared sniggered. He went through women faster than I did.

"I'm tasking you two with making sure it happens. We all have a lot to lose if Levi can't keep his pants on long enough to find a worthy girl."

"Absolutely, sir." Of course Owen agreed immediately. He'd been kissing my father's ass for years.

"Can we please talk about the real plan? The one that doesn't involve my sex life."

Dad leaned his elbows on his desk. He looked tired. "All we can do is stay alert and make sure our own ranks are loyal. If things come to blow, we can't have any mutiny from within."

"I'm guessing my dad's already on that?" Jared asked.

"Yes. But I expect you all to do your part."

"Will do, sir." Even Jared knew that pushing my dad could have dire consequences.

"Good. Now get out of here. I have better things to do today." He went back to the paperwork. I wondered if it was anything real, or just an excuse to look busy.

"Bye, Dad. Great talking to you." I got the hell out of his office and back to the elevator. I was angry, and I could feel the transformation wanting to happen. I relaxed and pushed it back. I had other things to think about, namely Miss Legs.

Chapter Two

I leaned back against the black leather couch in our house. I'd had the couch for two years, the same amount of time I'd lived in the place. As soon as freshman year ended, Jared, Owen, and I moved in there. One year in the dorms was more than enough for us.

With some distance, I was finally relaxing after the meeting with my dad. The man knew how to boil my blood, and it usually took time and copious amounts of alcohol to get back to normal. Nothing I did was ever good enough for him, and after twenty-two years, I was beyond tired of it.

"So where do you think those girls are?" I knew I was being ridiculous. There were plenty of attractive girls around, but there was something about her that got under my skin. I'd practically memorized every curve of her body in the seconds she'd been in view. She wouldn't be escaping from me so easily again.

Jared tossed me another beer from the fridge. "It's their first night in the French Quarter. They'll be at the Cat's Meow. They always go to the Cat's Meow."

"No way. She's not the type." I tried to picture her at a place like that. No, she was classier. She'd probably be looking for a lounge or something.

"Not the type?" Jared twisted off the top of his beer. "I guarantee they'll be there. I bet you fifty they'll sing karaoke."

Owen walked in, dumping three po' boys on the table. "Who? Those girls from the hotel? Yeah, I'm in on this. My bet is *Girl's Just Want to Have Fun*. They always sing that."

"No, I bet they're more the *Like a Virgin* types," Jared threw in.

"I'm game. But let's make it a hundred. I haven't washed either of you out in a while." Things were always more fun when there was money involved.

They both laughed. "All right, a hundred."

I dug into my shrimp po' boy, already planning out the evening. I'd find the girl and forget all about the bullshit with my dad.

The door burst open again, and the flash of red hair made it immediately clear who'd arrived.

"Have you ever heard of knocking?" Owen snapped at his little sister, Hailey.

"If you have a problem with it, lock the door." She swiped a Coke from the fridge. She had no problem making herself at home.

"Is there a reason you're gracing us with your presence?" I'd known Hailey her whole life and she was like a little sister—the annoying, won't ever leave you alone type. She was only three years younger than us, but sometimes it seemed like ten.

Hailey leaned back against the counter. "Yeah. I need Owen to talk to Dad."

"I doubt I'm going to, but about what?" Owen answered after finishing off his sandwich.

"He's making me request J.L. as a dorm. There is no way I'm living in an all-girls dorm!"

We all laughed. I still couldn't believe she was starting at Tulane in the fall. How was she old enough for college? I still pictured her playing with dolls even though one glance at her figure told you those days were long gone.

"Come on. This is so not fair." Hailey pouted. When she made faces like that, she only looked younger. I decided not to point it out to her. Giving her a hard time was fun, but you had to be careful not to push it too far. It wasn't worth her wrath.

"You can't be surprised." Owen tried to keep a straight face.

Hailey walked into the living room and took a seat on the arm of a couch. "So he caught me making out with a guy? It's not like I was sleeping with him."

Owen cringed, probably mentally picturing his sister hooking up with someone. "Hailey, Dad's always been protective. Inviting a guy over when they weren't home wasn't the smartest decision, but how could you be stupid enough to get caught? You always wait until you know they won't possibly come back." Owen said it snidely, but

I think he actually felt bad. Their parents definitely treated them differently.

"So you really won't talk to him?" she whined.

Owen crumpled up the wrapper of his po' boy. "Living in a girl's dorm isn't that bad. It's nicer than a lot of the others."

"I guess." She slid down from the arm to a couch cushion. "I hope I at least get a cool roommate."

"Me too, because then maybe you won't show up here uninvited all the time." I couldn't resist. She was so easy to annoy.

"And don't worry, Hailey. I'd be more than happy to visit your new friends anytime." Jared winked.

"Arrgh! You guys are useless. Thanks for nothing." She stormed out just the way she arrived.

Owen got up, pushing back his chair. "Seriously, how am I related to her?"

Jared collected our plates and brought them to the sink. No one would believe how much of a neat freak he was. "I don't know, she's hot and you're ugly as shit." He grinned.

"Don't even start."

I laughed. My roommates were definitely entertaining.

Chapter Three

"You better be ready to pay up," Owen taunted. We'd spent the better part of an hour searching the Quarter. After striking out at the classier lounges and bars, I didn't want to admit that my friends were probably right. I finally gave in, and we walked into the Cat's Meow. It had been a while since I'd dragged myself into that place. It's not like it was much worse than the rest of the Bourbon Street bars, but you also had to suffer through horrible singing. The current song was no exception.

I looked over toward the stage and, sure enough, there they were, singing *Girls Just Want to Have Fun*. I had really misread her, or maybe it was the friend who convinced her to come. "Fine, I'll get you your money later."

It's not like I cared about two hundred bucks. The important part was that I'd found the girl. Mmm, yes, and she was wearing a short skirt. So maybe singing wasn't her strong suit, but she looked good doing it.

I bought a beer and went ahead and got a shot for her. I had a feeling she was going to need it when she was done. There was something about her expression that said she wasn't having as much fun as she was pretending to. But I was. Hell, I was having a great time. That jean skirt was so short. I got a real nice view.

"Are you sure they're legal?" Leave it to Owen to ask such a dumb question.

"Yeah, they've got to be eighteen."

He frowned. "You sure? Do you really want to mess with jail bait?"

"Shit, Owen, they're not kids. They got in here, didn't they?" Jared argued.

I tried to ignore them. I was still enjoying my view.

"They could have fakes. But it's your problem, not mine."

"Exactly, go find your own. Or wait, you don't do girls anymore." Jared smirked.

"Shut the fuck up."

"Both of you shut up." The song ended, and I watched as the girls jumped off the stage. I waited until they separated to make my move.

She was definitely flustered, not even paying attention to where she was going. I walked directly into her path.

"You look like you could use this." I pushed the shot into her hand.

She looked up at me, and I saw the recognition in her eyes. She remembered me. She nodded and then downed the shot.

"What was that?" She coughed a little. I probably could have gotten her something tamer, but what would have been the fun in that?

"A jaeger shot." I laughed. "Feeling better?"

"Yeah. I can't believe I did that." She looked back over her shoulder, like she was making sure the stage was still there.

"It really wasn't so bad. It was more entertaining than if Cyndi Lauper performed it herself." Much more entertaining. I looked at her up close for the first time. I watched as a few drops of sweat ran down from her neck and disappeared into her tank top. She had a nicer chest than I originally thought. Add in her killer legs and she was hotter than any girl I'd ever seen.

"So, thanks for the shot, but I need to find my friend."

"Hey, you can't run off on me again." If she thought she was getting away this time, she had another thing coming. She was mine. "Besides, your friend appears to be unavailable."

Surprisingly, Jared didn't already have her in a corner somewhere. She was occupied by some guy who looked like he was in town for a conference. I knew the type. He was looking to score, have a story to run home with. The blonde was drunk enough he might just get lucky.

"Run off on you again? That implies we've run into each other before."

So she was going to play that game?

"I saw you at the Crescent City Hotel this afternoon, but you took off before I could say hello." I leaned in closer, using the blaring music as an excuse, even though I could hear perfectly well. Damn, she even smelled good. I didn't recognize the perfume—but it was light, the right kind.

"Oh, I didn't notice you."

It was time to act interested in her life. "You here for vacation?"

"I'm here for work, actually, at the hotel." She flipped some of her long brown hair off her shoulder.

"Are you around for the whole summer then?" Not the tourist I expected. If the sex was as good as I knew it would be, a longer stay could be convenient.

"Yeah, I'm here until I start school in the fall." So Owen wasn't completely off. She was probably fresh out of high school.

"All right, so where are you going to school?"

"Princeton." She tried to hide a smile. She was proud, but didn't want me to know it.

"Nice." Smart girls weren't necessarily bad, as long as they didn't overanalyze everything.

"You in school?"

"Yeah, I'm going to be a senior at Tulane." Maybe she'd loosen up a little if she realized I was in school. Some girls were like that. They assumed you were a good guy if you were in college. It made no sense, but it usually worked.

"Oh, so you live here?"

"Born and raised."

"I didn't think locals hung out at places like this."

"We don't usually, but they're great spots to meet girls from out of town." Or more specifically, it was a good spot to find her.

She shook her head. "Ah, so you're one of them."

"One of who?" I tried to figure out what group she was throwing me in with.

"The type to prey on innocent tourists."

"Innocent tourists? You make me sound like the big bad wolf."

"And you're not?" She got a twinkle in her eye.

A wolf? As if she was dealing with something that tame. "Only if you're Red Riding Hood." I'd pretend to be a wolf if it involved her.

"Wow, that's original," she said sarcastically, but her face gave her away. She was definitely interested. "Well, nice talking to you."

What? Was she seriously trying to blow me off again? I had to act fast. "Hey, I didn't even get your name yet."

"Allie."

"Is that short for Allison?" I needed to keep her talking.

"Yes, but no one calls me Allison."

"I'm Levi." I held out my hand.

"Is that short for something?" She gave me her hand and it felt nice in mine. I didn't want to end the contact. I liked touching her, but I finally dropped it.

"Leviathan. But you can call me whatever you like." Hell, she could call me a wolf if she was doing it in my bed.

"Well, nice to meet you." She actually started to walk away. What the hell was going on?

"Wow, it's hotel bar guy." The blonde swayed as she walked over drunkenly. Either she was a light weight or she'd had more to drink than Allie. Allie—it was nice to have a name to go with those long legs.

"So you did notice me." I leaned in closer to Allie again. If she'd noticed me enough to talk to her friend, I was good to go. She was just playing hard to get. I didn't mind a good game of chase.

"So, does that mean you changed your mind?" the blonde asked.

"Changed her mind? About what?" Had she talked about me more?

"Allie's sworn off men, or so she claims." Blondie took a swig from her beer. If she drank much more, she'd pass out before anyone got her home.

"Is that so?" What did that mean exactly? I'd have thought she was into girls, but I wasn't getting that vibe.

Allie exhaled loudly. "Yes, not that it's any of your business."

"Any particular reason why?" I was intrigued. Had someone hurt her? I felt an unfamiliar feeling of protectiveness take hold. I shook it off.

"None that I wish to explain."

"She thinks it's because she has bad luck with relationships, but really it's because no one is good enough for her," Blondie tattled. Allie's eyes got all big—I got myself ready for a cat fight.

But then Allie relaxed her shoulders. "I think I need another drink."

"My pleasure. What can I get you?"

"Surprise me." There was nothing overly flirtatious in her voice, but I still took her willingness to trust me with the task as a good sign.

"I will." I winked at her. "I'm good at surprises."

I needed to find the perfect drink. Allie seemed like the kind of girl who liked them strong and sweet. I ordered her something different, my own invention. I called it the Oasis. I heard the girls continuing to argue. One of the many benefits of enhanced hearing was eavesdropping in on conversations. The blonde's name was Jess, and she was really egging Allie on.

As I returned to the girls, Jared caught my eye. He and Owen were sitting at a table across the room. He nodded, wanting us to come over. Normally, I'd have made him get off his ass, but I wanted Allie's attention, which meant getting her friend fixated on someone else.

"A few of my friends are sitting over there. Care to join us?"

Jess glanced over and answered first. "Why not?" Her words were casual but it was obvious she was interested in one of my friends. I hoped it was Owen—that would make tonight interesting.

Allie still hadn't said anything, so I looked to her. She finally nodded, and we walked over.

I made the introductions. "Girls, this is Jared and Owen. And this is Allie and Jess." I realized afterward that they might have thought it was odd that I knew Jess' name, but they didn't seem to notice.

"Well, hello there." Jared grinned. He looked over Allie, but then moved his attention to Jess.

Owen just nodded. "Hey." He smiled again, but I didn't worry about it. He knew not to get in the way of what I wanted.

Jess sat down next to Jared. He must have been the one who caught her eye. I'd hoped she'd keep Owen occupied so he'd stop looking at Allie, but it didn't actually matter.

I put down our drinks and pulled out a chair for Allie, careful to make sure she sat in the one closest to the wall. I wanted her attention all to myself. "You can't really mean to punish the entire male gender for the errors of a few."

I watched her pick up her drink and taste it. Her whole body responded to the sip. Her shoulders relaxed and she leaned back against her chair. She liked it, and I liked her smile. It went all the way to her eyes.

"Because it would be really unfair to do that."

"Um, can we please talk about something else?" She turned away from me, and I saw her looking at Owen. Not what I was hoping for.

"Sure, for now. What made you decide to take the job at the hotel?"

Her shoulders tensed up a little again. "Oh, I needed a job and my dad was able to get it for me."

Jess leaned over the table toward me. "Because Allie's dad is super rich and bought the place." Whoa. This was the new owner's daughter? I wasn't sure what to make of the information. "What? It's true."

I must have missed an exchange between the girls. Was Allie trying to keep it a secret? Most girls would brag about something like that.

"Your dad bought the Crescent City Hotel?" Jared sat up straighter. He seriously needed to keep his cool.

"Yeah. The deal went through earlier this year." Allie downed her drink. Something about this conversation was stressing her out. I wanted to find out what it was. I doubted she knew anything about the hotel. It was something else.

I wasn't about to ask her about it. I'd just have to find out another way. She set down her empty glass.

"I guess you liked it?"

"Maybe a little. What was it?" She ran her finger over the edge of the glass.

"Want another?"

"No, don't worry about it. I can get one for myself if you'll tell me what it is." I could practically see the wheels turning in her head. She was the type of girl who worried about guys buying her drinks. She was afraid that meant she owed them something. Such bullshit. Buying a drink for a girl was just an opening. Where it went after that depended on her.

"I'm getting up anyway. Besides, if you don't know what it is, you'll have to let me keep buying them for you." I enjoyed the look of annoyance that flashed across her face. I pushed back my chair without giving her a chance to argue.

"Don't worry. She's not always so uptight." Jess' voice surprised me as I ordered some more drinks. I hadn't expected Jared and Jess to follow me. That left Allie alone with Owen—not the plan—definitely not the plan.

"I'm not worried about it," I said offhandedly, wanting the bartender to move faster. This was taking far too long. Owen was laughing. What could she be saying? At least she didn't look as amused.

"Levi's good at, uh, breaking through tough exteriors." Jared ordered them a couple of shots.

"She's worth it," Jess said as I walked away. I couldn't read Jess. One moment she was egging her friend on and the next she was talking her up. I ignored the comment and kept walking. I'd been away from the table long enough.

"It looked like you two were having a good conversation. Did I miss anything?" I shot Owen an annoyed look. He was seriously beginning to piss me off.

Allie glanced up at me. "Nothing worth repeating."

Owen smiled. "Well, Allie was telling me that she isn't interested in you."

Hmm, well at least they were talking about me.

I took my seat and leaned in close to her, letting her know what I thought of the statement. "It's because she's sworn off men. But I think I'll just have to be the exception."

She took a few sips of the new drink. "What in the world would make you think that you would be an exception?"

"One, you're attracted to me, and two, I can be very persistent."

She tightened her grip on the glass. "I am not attracted to you!"

"Like hell you're not," Jess said before bursting into laughter. She hadn't even sat down yet.

"You know there could be a few females alive that aren't into you, Levi," Jared mocked. I was ready to knock that smirk off his face.

"It's always a possibility, but that's not the case this time. She likes me, she just won't admit it." I scooted my chair closer to her.

She sighed and closed her eyes. She seemed pretty stressed out, and I wanted to do something about that. I put an arm around her shoulder. It felt nice, natural.

I moved close enough that I could kiss her, but I resisted. It wasn't time yet. She moved to turn away but I caught her chin, making her look up at me. "Stop looking away. I love green eyes."

"Does that line usually work for you?"

"Usually. I'm guessing it's not going to work tonight."

Her lips quirked into just a hint of a smile. "Not a chance."

"I'll just have to get more creative." As frustrating as her resistance was, it was also a nice change of pace. It would make finally getting her in bed all the more worth it.

"You do that." Her look was teasing. She was definitely challenging me.

"So, what do you think of New Orleans so far?" Owen asked her, having to pull her attention away again.

Jess answered. "It's been fantastic. It's so awesome to get away and meet new people."

"And what about you, Allie?" I asked, finding I actually cared about her answer.

"Well, considering we've been here less than twenty-four hours, it's hard to have much of an impression, but I like it so far."

I leaned in again. "You'll have to keep me posted as you have more time to form an opinion."

"I'll be sure to keep you updated."

I thought there might be a promise in her words, but that might have just been wishful thinking. The game of chase was fun, but I was ready to move things forward.

"You girls want to see the rest of the Quarter?" Jared was just looking for an excuse to get Jess to leave with him. The conference guy from earlier was watching her. She didn't seem to notice. Jared definitely had her attention.

"Yes!" Jess squeaked. "We haven't seen anything but here and the hotel."

"You interested?" I whispered in Allie's ear. I liked how it made her shiver a little. I definitely had an effect on her.

"Sure. Why not?" She finished off her drink and stood up. She tugged down on her skirt. I had to resist the urge to reach out and stop her. The skirt was fine the way it was.

I put an arm around her, leading her out. I shot Owen a backward glance to let him know to stay away. "I guarantee you're going to love New Orleans."

She slipped away from me. I held in a frustrated sigh.

"Is that right?" She sounded distracted, and I noticed her staring at her friend and Jared. Was she worried about her?

We walked down St. Peter Street and crossed over into Jackson Square. Allie seemed entranced by it. I noticed her eyeing the wrought iron railings. That was the second time I'd noticed her admiring architecture. Maybe we had that interest in common.

We maneuvered through the square, past the usual crowd of musicians and artists showing off their work.

"Care to have your fortune read?" a palm reader called out.

"No, thanks." Allie waved her off.

I let my arm brush against hers. "Are you sure you don't want a glimpse into your future?"

"I prefer surprises." Her response seemed at odds with how uptight she'd been most of the night. I sensed there was a lot more to her I still wasn't seeing.

"Same here," Jess agreed. "This is too cool. It might be even better than Washington Square Park."

Washington Square? So they were New Yorkers.

"Of course, this is just where all the tourists hang out. There are much cooler places, hon. Maybe I'll show you sometime," Jared crooned.

"Like where, your apartment?" Allie raised an eyebrow. She had a nice sense of humor.

"Why, you want to see my place?" he threw back at her.

"In your dreams."

I laughed. She had some nerve. I couldn't resist touching her. I came up from behind her and wrapped my arms around her waist. She fit perfectly. "Would you change your mind about that if you knew I was his roommate?"

"Why would that change my mind?" She pushed away. I reluctantly released her.

Maybe I needed to give her space so she'd come to me. Her game was wearing on me, but it was only going to end one way. With her in my bed.

I tried to pay attention to everything else going on, but then, of course, Owen had to go talk to her again. Pushing my annoyance aside, I listened in. They were talking about a crow on the fence. She seemed to find the bird creepy, and I wondered what she'd think if she knew what I was. When I heard them talking about going home, I had to intervene. She was thanking Owen for giving her a heads up.

"The heads up on what?"

"I was simply suggesting she pry Jess away from Jared if she wants to get her home tonight."

"What's the hurry? The night is young." I smiled at her, resisting the urge to punch Owen. If I wasn't good at controlling myself, my eyes would have changed.

"We have our first day of work tomorrow."

"Your first day of work at your father's hotel. Can't you skip out?" I was definitely not ready to say goodnight, and it was looking unlikely she was coming home with me.

"No! I am not missing my first day of work. I'm not like that."

If I couldn't have her that night, I'd just have to try again. "Really? Maybe I can learn more about you tomorrow night? Maybe over dinner?"

"Not a chance."

"Oh, that's right; you think you've sworn off men."

She pretended to ignore me, but I saw the tiny curl of her lips. "Jess, let's go!"

"Now? Seriously?" Jess whined.

"I'm sure you can meet up with your friend another time."

Her friend? Allie had a bit of edge, didn't she?

"What's the rush all of a sudden?" Jared asked, glaring at Allie.

"Owen decided to point out the late hour to her." I knew Jared would appreciate it as much as I did.

"What the hell, man?" Jared lunged at Owen, his eyes turning black. I hoped the girls didn't notice, and I put myself between my friends. We'd have to settle this later.

"Let it go, Jared. I'm sure we'll have plenty of opportunities to see them again. We'll walk you girls home." I wasn't happy to see Allie leave, but I also wanted another chance. It was time to cut our losses and regroup.

When we reached the hotel, Allie waved. "Goodnight."

"I'll be seeing you," I said before walking away. I'm sure she had no clue how true my words were—there wasn't a chance in the world I was letting this girl go.

Chapter Four

Miraculously, Jared didn't kill Owen. Jared was usually reasonable, but if you cock blocked him, you needed to be ready for his wrath. They'd stopped fighting long enough to go to sleep, but that didn't mean Jared wasn't still angry the next day. I poured myself a cup of coffee and watched as they stared each other down in the kitchen.

"Are you guys going to survive if I leave for a few hours?" I wasn't in a rush to go anywhere, but I didn't have a choice.

"If you're going to stalk that girl from last night, I'm going to have to intervene." Jared laughed.

"I'm not stalking anyone." Even if I did want to see her again. "My grandparents are in town. I've been ordered to attend a family lunch at my parents' house."

"Oh. Lucky you." Jared popped open the top on a can of Coke. "I'd offer to join you, but I'd rather go to the dentist."

"Your family isn't that bad." Owen seemed relieved Jared had moved on from threatening his life. "If you need company, I'll suffer along with you."

"I appreciate the sacrifice, but that's not going to fly with Georgina." My grandmother was pretty intense, and a family lunch was limited to family. No exceptions.

"Call us when you get out."

"If I get out," I mumbled as I walked to the door. "Try not to kill each other while I'm gone."

Jared laughed. "I'm over it. We'll go out later and find someone else."

"Yeah, maybe." I left before he could question me. I was already late to see my family. I didn't feel like explaining to my friends that I didn't want to find another girl. Until I got Allie into bed, no one else was going to cut it.

I parked my black BMW along the curb in front of my parents' large white house. With a wraparound porch and tall columns, it fit the southern style you would expect to see in the Garden District. After sitting in the car longer than necessary, I got out and headed to the front door. There was no reason to further delay the inevitable, and hopefully the afternoon would go by quickly.

My mom opened the door before I could ring the bell. I still had a key, but I never used it anymore. "Hey, honey." The stress on her face could only mean one thing. Georgina had already arrived.

"Hi, Mom. Sorry I'm late."

"It's fine."

"It's fine?" My grandmother strode into the entryway. Tall and always impeccably dressed, my grandmother was nothing like most women her age. She was so full of energy and ready to jump on any mistake, she could intimidate any woman or man. My grandfather was included in that. I guess some might find it comical that the former King of the Society was terrified of his very human wife.

"Hi, Grandma. Sorry about that."

"It's all right, Leviathan. You learned your manners from your mother. I can't blame you." She gave me a light hug while glaring at my mom.

"It's not Mom's fault."

"Sure. Maybe not this time."

Mom gave me a "don't make it worse" look. I nodded. She was right. Nothing I could say was going to make it better. Besides, she'd start in on me soon enough.

"Where's Dad?" I assumed he was in his study, but I figured it was worth asking. Escaping from Georgina's eye for a few minutes was usually worth facing my father alone.

"He's working. Let's talk." Georgina took my arm and led me toward the living room. My mother didn't follow. I didn't blame her.

I took a seat in a beige arm chair. Georgina sat down caddy corner on a matching couch.

"How was your trip?" I decided to start with the niceties. That would give her less time to grill me about my life.

"Don't bother, Leviathan. We both know why I'm here."

I grinned. "To spend time with your adoring family?"

30

"I take it you haven't made any more progress with finding a mate?" She leaned forward slightly.

I exhaled loudly. "What's the rush?"

"What's the rush? As though you don't know the consequences if you fail to have an heir."

I pictured what I'd get to do with Allie to make an heir. I quickly pushed that thought away. I was only a few feet from my grandmother. "I'll have a kid eventually."

"You've met someone." Her lips curved into a small smile. "Out with it."

"What?" I sat up with a start. Had I said something out loud?

She cast me a warning glance. "Don't lie to me. You were day dreaming about someone."

"I don't day dream."

"I expect to meet her soon." She folded her hands in her lap.

"There's no one to meet." I didn't even have a real date lined up with Allie, and I was thinking about getting her into bed, not binding her to me as my lifelong mate.

"If there's no one, would you like me to introduce you to a few candidates? I know of several young women who might be worthy of your hand."

"No!" I shot up out of my chair. There was no way my grandmother was playing matchmaker. "I'll pick my own mate."

"Then do it." She stood and hugged me again. As she turned to leave the room, she whispered, "You'll know it if you find her." Her voice was low, but she wanted me to hear. I didn't need to listen to any of that again.

I suffered through lunch. My grandmother only criticized my mother's cooking once, but the conversation was awkward and no one wanted to be there. My father barely said two words to me. I knew he was still pissed about me missing the meeting. As soon as I finished, I excused myself from the table and went up to my childhood bedroom.

The room was sparsely furnished and decorated, exactly the way it had been when I was a kid. My father didn't believe that boys should bother with anything but the basics. Toys and posters would only get in the way. I walked past my king sized bed, still covered in the blue comforter I'd grown up with, before stopping in front of my dresser. I pulled open my sock drawer and searched around until I found the small ring. I'd freaked out when my father gave me the ring that was intended for my mate. Seven years later and the ruby-covered ring still scared me. I ran my fingers over the stones, stuffing it in my pocket when I heard a knock on the door.

I turned to face my mom in the doorway. "Hey, Mom." She was the one member of the family I actually got along with.

"You doing all right up here? You were really quiet at lunch." Her warm eyes studied my face. She was worried about me.

"Am I ever talkative at these things?"

She strode over to me. "No, but you're going to be king soon. You're going to have to get better at controlling your feelings."

"And I need to find a mate. Isn't that what the theme of the day is?"

"No. You don't need to find a mate." She gave me a long look.

"I don't?" That was news.

"You need to find the right mate." She patted me on the shoulder. "Think about that."

"Is it okay if I leave?"

"Sure. Just slip out the back."

"Thanks." I gave her a quick hug before taking the back stairs two at a time. It wasn't until I was in my car that I realized I hadn't put the ring back.

Chapter Five

I owed Jared. Short of stalking the hotel to look for her or talking to my contacts, I had no immediate way to see Allie again. Lucky for me, Jess had happily slipped her number to Jared. All it took was one phone call, and the plans were set. From what I gathered, Allie hadn't been part of the planning, but that didn't worry me. She could play hard to get all she wanted. At the end of the night, she'd be coming home with me.

We waited in front of the elevators. I'd never picked up a girl at the hotel before, but my assumption was they weren't taking the stairs down. After waiting a few minutes, the doors opened, and I remembered why I was putting in all the effort. Allie looked even hotter than last time. She wore a pink halter style dress that accentuated her green eyes. Like everything else I'd seen her in, it was short, and she kept it casual with flip-flops. I liked that she wasn't the kind of girl who wore heels all the time. Heels could be hot, but a pair of flip-flops meant a girl was laid back.

"Hey there, Allison." I purposely used her full name to see what kind of response I got.

"It's Allie." She feigned annoyance, but I noticed her studying my chest and arms.

I smiled, letting her know I'd caught her in the act of checking me out. "Oh yeah, I forgot."

"I'm sure." She shook her head, bringing my attention to her hair. I wanted to run my hands through those brown locks. I also wanted them sprawled out on my pillow.

"Are you girls ready to see uptown?" Owen addressed both of them. I got the sense he was being careful. Smart guy.

Allie adjusted her purse on her shoulder. "Sure, should we follow you or get an address for my GPS?"

"Neither." I put a hand on the small of her back and led her toward the door. "We're taking the streetcar. That way you don't have to worry about a designated driver."

"Will it still be running when we need to get home?" She seemed worried. Wasn't she from New York? Did New Orleans at night scare her that much? She didn't need to worry about anything with me around.

"This is New Orleans. It runs all night." Jared didn't bother to sugar coat his annoyance at her. He wasn't an Allie fan for some reason, but it wasn't my problem.

I stayed close to Allie's side as we walked the few blocks to the corner of Canal and St. Charles. We caught the streetcar just before it pulled away. Allie struggled to slip a dollar bill into the machine, and I pushed her hand away.

She wasn't paying for anything when she was with me. "I've got this."

The car lurched forward and Allie lost her balance. I caught her easily in my arms. "Easy does it, darling." I inhaled her warm sweet scent. She wore the same perfume again. After detangling herself from my arms, she held onto the seats as she walked down the aisle. She'd barely settled into a seat when I slid in right next to her.

"So where are we going exactly?" She looked over me to watch Jess and Jared. I may have had my work cut out for me, but Jared had a guarantee going for him.

I pulled her attention away from them. "The Maple Leaf. It's a bar that always has great live music. You're going to like it."

She rested a hand on her leg. "Glad to know you are now an expert on what I like."

"I'm an expert on a lot of things." I stretched out my legs, brushing my leg against hers in the process. Her body tensed ever so slightly, but it wasn't in a bad way.

She gazed out the window, and I was glad it was a clear night out. The windows on the streetcar were open, providing a nice breeze. I needed it with the way my body heated around her. She felt it too. I know she did. There was an electricity sizzling between us like nothing I'd ever experienced before. I wanted her so bad it hurt.

I followed her gaze. She was checking out the houses lining St. Charles. "Beautiful, aren't they?" I leaned in close and smiled when I noticed the goose bumps forming on her exposed shoulder. Considering the heat, I knew I was the cause of them.

She took a moment to answer. "The homes? Yeah, they're gorgeous. Is this the Garden district?"

"Yes. Home sweet home."

"Have you always lived here?" she asked absently, probably deciding which house she'd want for herself.

"Born and raised, and I never want to move anywhere else." I also had no choice. New Orleans would always be my home.

She turned away from the window and her face was mere inches from mine. "Really?"

I fought the urge to taste her lips. I couldn't rush the moment and lose my chance. "Does that really surprise you?"

"I mean, you told me you were from here, but don't most people our age want to explore new places?"

If she only knew how tied to New Orleans I was. At the moment, I couldn't have cared less where I was though. The company was all I needed. "Why explore when you have everything you need right here?"

"Yeah. Whatever." She turned away again, but I didn't miss her lingering glance. I let her enjoy the view until we reached our stop.

I touched her leg gently. "This is us." I pulled the cord to request a stop, then I led her off the car. "It's just a few blocks from here."

We'd only made it a few steps when Jess walked between us and grabbed Allie's hand. "Have a nice ride?"

"Splendid." Allie's face was slightly flushed.

Jess grinned. "It looked like you were enjoying yourself."

I laughed. Obviously, I wasn't the only one who picked up on it.

Allie gave it right back to her. "Yeah, I wouldn't have thought you noticed. You looked pretty distracted yourself."

"Unlike you, I'm not going to pretend otherwise." Jess smiled again before pulling Allie along with her to catch up with Jared. Man, he had her interested.

I pushed open the door to one of my favorite bars. The Maple Leaf doesn't look particularly special on the outside, but the music and overall feel of the place made it worth coming back to. I headed straight through to the back patio, checking behind me to make sure Allie was still with me.

"Owen!" Hailey noticed us immediately and decided to annoy the hell out of Owen by pulling him into a hug.

I laughed to myself as he quickly broke away. "Aww, damn it, Hailey. I should have known you would be here."

"Don't bother hiding it, Owen. You know you're glad to see your favorite sister." She grinned.

"You mean my only sister."

Hailey quickly lost interest in Owen when she noticed the girls. "Hi. I don't think we've met." She held out her hand.

Allie accepted her handshake. "I'm Allie."

Hailey moved on to Jess next.

Hailey smiled at Jess before turning her attention to Allie again. "Nice to meet you. So you're friends with my brother then?"

Allie's brow furrowed slightly. "Sort of…"

"Enough of the twenty questions. We met them down at the hotel. Allie's dad owns the place now," Owen explained.

"Oh!" Hailey caught the glare I shot her and recovered quickly. Letting the girls know there was anything important about the hotel wouldn't be a good thing.

"Watch it, Hailey," Jared warned.

Hailey nodded at us both. She understood. "It's really nice to meet you both. My best friends deserted me to spend the summer abroad, and I could really use some other girls around."

"Wait, Beth and Jill both left already? Who are you here with?" Owen pretended not to care, but he was still her big brother.

"I came by myself to meet up with Jamie. Not a big deal."

"Oh, okay, but don't leave by yourself."

"Like I can't take care of myself?" She put a hand on her hip.

"Just humor me, Hailey."

"Sure." She rolled her eyes. "God, older brothers can be annoying. Do you have any siblings, Allie?"

"Nope, I'm an only child."

Interesting. It looked we had something in common.

39

"So lucky," Jess broke in. "I have four younger brothers and sisters."

"Four? Wow," Hailey was probably picturing having to deal with more than one Owen.

Jess nodded. "Yeah, I know. Thankfully, I was always able to escape the chaos by crashing at Allie's because her mom is cool. She's so lucky."

"My mom is pretty cool." Allie seemed to be lost in thought for a minute. I wondered what the story was. She'd mentioned her dad bought the hotel, but from what I knew, there wasn't a Mrs. around.

Satisfied she wasn't going anywhere, I slipped back inside to get us some drinks. There was a line at the bar, but the bartender served me immediately. I didn't know him by name, but he definitely knew who I was. I ordered myself an Abita and decided to go with another Oasis for Allie. She seemed to like the last two. I listened to the band for a few seconds before heading back outside. Allie was exactly where I left her.

"I got your drink for you." I held out her glass.

She seemed surprised. I guess she hadn't noticed my absence. "My drink?"

"You seemed to like it the other night."

"And you still aren't going to tell me what's in it?"

"Nope." No reason to reveal any of my cards yet.

"Well, there are other ways of figuring it out." She gave me a coy smile.

"Are there now?" Now this was good. Things were finally moving in the right direction.

"Uh-huh." Damn, a girl like that shouldn't be allowed to look at a man that way. My jeans weren't going to be my friend for long.

"You care to share?"

"Not right now." She smiled and took a seat next to Owen. I stifled the growl I felt rising in my throat. To make matters worse, Hailey jumped into the empty seat next to her before I got the chance. That girl was looking for trouble. I shot her a dirty look. Jess let out a giggle. She was perched on Jared's lap. He looked very pleased with the arrangement.

The table was also occupied by a few guys I knew from Society events. One of them immediately jumped out of his seat and offered it to me.

"That won't be necessary. I'm sure Allie and I can share." I looked right at her. If she was going to eye fuck me, I was going to do it right back.

"You wish."

"Why? You afraid you might actually like it?" I taunted. I was getting frustrated. She obviously wanted me too. Why was she being so difficult?

She shivered, and I loved that I had that effect on her. "Not a chance."

She stormed off inside. I gave her a few seconds head start before following her. She didn't notice. Instead, she got distracted by the music. I watched her body move to the beat, completely oblivious to anyone or anything around her. My body rebelled at the thought of her so unprotected. Where was this coming from? She was just a girl.

I ordered her another Oasis and waited until I saw her set aside her empty glass at the bar before approaching again. I leaned against the bar, waiting for her to notice. "I told you you'd like it here."

She turned to look up at me. "I admit it's pretty cool. Who is this, by the way?"

"Oh, it's the Rebirth Brass Band. Heard of them?"

"I don't think so, but that isn't surprising. I'm not exactly up on the New Orleans music scene. Anyway, what was that all about back there?"

"What do you mean?"

"Why do people act like you walk on water or something?"

"How do you know I don't?" I handed her the drink. She accepted it with a nod and took a long slow sip. My eyes went to her lips, so ready to know what they felt like. I was tired of waiting.

"Don't what?"

"Walk on water."

"Wow, you are even cockier than I thought."

I laughed. She really said what was on her mind.

"All right, I can't walk on water, but I can do other things very, very well." And I was ready to show her exactly what I meant.

"Oh yeah?" She licked her lip, and I knew she was thinking the same thoughts as me.

"Let me show you." I leaned in and brushed my lips against hers gently, just long enough for her to think I wasn't going to take it further. Without warning, I picked it up, crushing my lips into hers. She responded, and I wrapped her up in my arms, devouring the sweet taste of her mouth as her hands twisted in my hair. Every inch of me was on fire, begging for more. There was something special about her, and one kiss was definitely not going to be enough.

I heard someone clear their throat, bringing me back to where we were. I reluctantly broke the kiss. "Still going to pretend you aren't interested, Allison?"

She gazed up at me with this dazed expression. I laughed. "I told you to call me Allie."

"You said everyone calls you Allie. I'm not everyone." She wasn't going to be able to keep me at bay. Any chance of staying away from me was over the second my lips touched hers.

"Are you always this frustrating?"

"Depends on who you ask."

She groaned before setting aside her partially full glass. I followed her back out onto the patio. I was still on a high from the kiss and just trying to come up with the best way to ask her home. She wanted to, but I had the feeling she was still going to resist.

I sat watching her for hours. She seemed so comfortable hanging out with my friends, and she especially seemed to be hitting it off with Hailey. I liked that. Why? Why did I care if a girl I slept with was friends with my roommate's little sister? Because I wanted her to stick around. The thought hit me like a strike of lightning. Forget a few nights, I wanted this girl longer.

I zoned out most of their conversation, trying to keep my mind off the kiss and the growing bulge in my pants, by discussing college sports with Jared. Eventually, I got pulled back into their conversation. Somehow the topic of action movies had come up.

"Okay, so who would win in a fight, Jean-Claude Van Damme, Stephen Segal, Bruce Lee, or Jackie Chan?" Owen asked.

"Easy, Jean-Claude. I mean he's hot and bad ass. Can you get any better?" Allie answered animatedly.

"Wait, so I'm not the only 18-year-old Jean-Claude fan? Nice!" Hailey gave her a high five.

"That's who you find hot?" I smirked. "But anyway, Owen, you left out Chuck Norris."

"Please, no. Someone stop Levi from starting in on Chuck Norris. There are only so many of those jokes I can take." Hailey hit the table with her hand and spilled several of the drinks. For some reason, the girls thought this was funny, and they started cracking up. Allie had a great smile and an even better laugh.

"Wow, is it really 2:30?" She squinted at the face of her watch. She blinked a few times before pulling out a small bottle from her purse and putting in some eye drops. She must have had contacts. I couldn't relate. I had perfect vision.

"Did you guys drive?" Hailey asked.

44

"No, we took the streetcar." Allie yawned.

"Why don't you guys come back to our place? It's really late anyhow," Jared suggested.

"That sounds like a great idea." Jess ran her hand down Jared's leg.

Allie didn't hide her distaste at the idea. I tried not to let that irk me. "I'm sure it does, Jess."

"I'd have to agree." I smiled. She had to be messing with me. There was no way she wanted to go home.

"I'd invite you guys to crash at my house, but my parents will flip if they see that I've been drinking. I'm going to stay over at their place anyway," Hailey explained.

"You still live at home?" Allie seemed surprised.

"Yeah. I just graduated from high school."

"Oh, duh. You said you were eighteen. Okay, I'll stay at their place then." For some reason, knowing that Hailey was coming made the prospect more appealing to Allie. I'd have to remember to thank Hailey later.

Chapter Six

"I knew I'd be taking you home tonight," I whispered as we walked toward our house. The night was warm, even at the late hour. There was no escaping the heat during the summer in New Orleans. Lucky for me, my body easily adjusted to any temperature. Unfortunately, that self-regulation didn't apply to the effect Allie had on me. One touch from her had me burning up.

She continued to play hard to get and shrugged my arm off her shoulder. I laughed. Now that I had the physical evidence of her interest, I wasn't as worried. That kiss had spoken volumes. She wanted me, and she wanted me bad.

I unlocked the front door, ushering Allie in before following closely behind her. She gazed around our living room as Jared led a giggling Jess down the hall to his room. Allie made a face when she noticed it out of the corner of her eye. She didn't try to stop her friend, but I sensed she wanted to. My guess is she was used to Jess' behavior. The girl wasn't drunk. Jared wasn't a complete asshole. We both had the same rule when it came to women. If they weren't sober enough to completely consent, then we let them go. There were plenty of girls to go around. Except I didn't feel that way that night. I didn't want anyone but Allie.

Allie seemed uptight. She took a seat on one of the leather couches, keeping her legs pressed firmly together. I wondered if the position was intentional, or if it was her subconscious attempt at resisting me. I sat down right next to her. I needed to put her at ease. She seemed most comfortable when I hit on her. I decided to go with it.

She blinked and yawned silently.

"You are more than welcome to sleep in my bed." I put my feet up on the circular ottoman.

"As tempting as that offer is, I'll take my chances out here." She took off her flip-flops and curled her legs up on the couch under her. I fought the urge to pull her legs onto my lap. I'd have given her a foot rub if she'd wanted one. I'm definitely not a foot guy, but every part of Allie seemed worth exploring.

"Wow, Levi, you've never offered to let me take your bed before." Hailey feigned hurt.

"And I'll never offer you my bed. If you don't want to sleep on the couch, talk to your brother, or better yet, go home."

"Aww, you are always so sweet to me."

Allie laughed. My plan was working. She was relaxing. Owen took a seat on the couch across from us, and Hailey entertained Allie with stories of how much trouble we used to get into as kids. Before long, Allie's head slumped down on my shoulder.

Owen nodded to where she rested. "Looks like we bored her to death."

"Nah, she's just tired. Humans need more sleep than us." Hailey stretched.

"Are you going to wake her up?" Owen asked.

"No. I'll let her sleep." I ran a hand down her arm. She was so sweet all curled up that way against me. "Get me the extra quilt in my closet and you can take my room tonight, Hailey."

She stood up. "Where are you going to sleep?"

"Right here."

Owen laughed. "You've got it bad."

"She's comfortable, and besides, I don't want her to wake up confused about where she is."

"Sure. Tell yourself whatever it takes." Owen started toward his room. "Night, guys."

Hailey tossed the quilt down on the ottoman. "Be good, Levi. I like her."

"Yeah, so do I. Considering I'm giving up my room, I wouldn't worry."

"That's what worries me…"

I laughed. "Get out of here."

As Hailey disappeared down the hall, I kicked off my shoes and repositioned us so we were lying down together. I gave her body a long look before covering us both up with the quilt.

I cuddled her in my arms, trying to tune out the sounds of Jared and Jess down the hall. Normally, I'd be jealous he was getting some when I wasn't, but I wouldn't have traded places for anything. I'd never just lay down with a girl like that before, but I liked it. Her breathing was even, and the pattern of it relaxed me. I closed my eyes, leaning back into a throw pillow. I thought about our kiss, the taste of her, and how perfectly her body felt pressed against mine. The thought started to get me hard in the wrong place, so I tried to push it out of my head. There was no reason to get excited. Tonight wasn't the night, but it would happen.

Another image flashed through my mind. Another night, a fireplace and a skylight open to the stars. I forced my eyes open. I couldn't go there. That was a thought that could only hurt me. Still, there was something about this girl that got to me, and I knew it wasn't just about sex. If it was, I wouldn't have been so satisfied just holding her. I stayed awake for hours listening to her breathe. I relaxed completely, and I felt strangely comfortable considering the cramped space. Finally, my body protested to the late hour, and I kissed her cheek before drifting off to sleep.

***

My body was stiff, but I'd never woken up in such a good mood before. Allie was snuggled up flush against me, and her hair and hands were sprawled across my chest. I imagined how much better the morning would be if we weren't wearing clothes, but somehow I was okay with the current situation.

She stirred, quietly at first, before doing this adorable stretch with her arms. She seemed to notice the cramped space and opened her eyes.

"Good morning, beautiful."

She clutched the blanket against her. "Oh god."

"Sleep well?"

She blinked a few times and looked around. "What are you doing here?"

"You're in my apartment, or did you forget?" I liked saying that.

"I mean why are you sleeping on the couch with me? Why aren't you in your room?"

"Oh, I gave my bed to Hailey."

"But I thought you'd never…"

"I was just messing with her. Besides, I thought we could use the privacy." I couldn't resist egging her on.

"Was I really so zonked out I missed all of this?"

"You fell asleep in the middle of a conversation and were leaning against me. You looked too comfortable to disturb, so I just moved us a bit." I left out asking Hailey for a blanket. She didn't need to know I'd actually put thought into the arrangement.

"I see. Well, at least we're on the couch and not your bed."

"Don't sound so relieved about it." I tried to sound playful, but would it have been so bad if we'd spent the night in my room?

"Hmm, yeah, because it would have felt great to wake up in bed with a guy I don't know."

"You do know me, Allison." Her name felt like velvet on my tongue. I knew she didn't like it, but I liked the way it riled her up. Besides, I was serious about not calling her what everyone else did.

"That again?" She shifted around. I knew she was trying to get up, but I wasn't quite ready to let go yet.

"You are really cute when you get angry."

"Just shut up and let go of me so I can get the heck out of here."

"Wow, calm down. Aren't you going to let me make you breakfast? It's the least I can do for the girl I just spent the night with."

"I did not spend the night with you. We were on the couch." She blinked again. I'd have to make sure she brought a case for her contacts next time she spent the night at my place. The next time. That thought got me excited.

"You spent the night in my arms, sweetheart. Sex or no sex, you can't argue that."

She groaned just as Owen walked into the room. He always had impeccable timing. I moved my arm so Allie could sit up. She smoothed out her dress and stood.

"Good morning. Did you enjoy the wonderful accommodations of our living room?"

"Where's Jess? Please tell me she's here somewhere." Allie's voice was a mix of worry and embarrassment. She didn't need to feel either. Jared wouldn't have hurt Jess, and she'd slept with me on the couch. What was embarrassing about that?

"She's in with Jared," Owen and I answered at the same time.

"Um, could one of you please get her for me?" She picked up her purse off the ground and put back on her flip-flops. Was she really just going to leave like that?

I couldn't get upset about it. I had no reason to. I'd just take her out again and end the night in my bed next time. But maybe I could stall her awhile longer. "There's no way I'm taking the chance of seeing Jared naked." I stretched in an exaggerated way to let her know I wasn't in any hurry.

She scrunched up her face. "Gross. Fine. Which room is his?"

"Seriously?"

"Yes, seriously. We have to be at work in like twenty minutes."

Again about work? Maybe her dad was as much of a hard ass as mine. Even so, I still had to try to get her to stay awhile. "Well, if you are already going to be late, you might as well stay for breakfast."

"Which room is his?" She repeated.

Owen pointed and she marched down the hall. A few minutes later, she opened the front door with Jess chasing after her. She was busy fidgeting with her sandals as Allie stepped outside. "You could have at least let me get dressed!"

Allie didn't respond. She only threw her an annoyed look. Even her annoyed look was cute. I was losing it.

"Thanks for an amazing night, Allison!" I laughed, enjoying her reaction to everything. She was the cutest thing I'd ever seen. And the hottest.

The girls were still arguing as they stepped into a cab.

Jared walked out of his room in just a pair of pajama pants. "Lovely morning, isn't it?"

I ignored him and started to make a pot of coffee.

"What's gotten into him?" Jared hopped up on the island counter.

"He spent the night on the couch." Owen took a bite out of an apple.

"Wait? You gave up your room to the girl and didn't join her?" The huge smirk on Jared's face said it all.

"No. He spent the night on the couch with her."

"With clothes on?" Jared raised an eyebrow.

"Yes." I was tired of letting Owen answer for me.

Jared cracked up. "Seriously? You slept with the girl on the couch?"

"Her name's Allie." I may have called her Allison to her face, but I didn't want Jared calling her that too.

"Well, I definitely didn't just sleep on the couch with her friend."

"Yeah. We heard." Hailey walked into the kitchen.

"Too much for your innocent ears?" Jared smirked.

"Do you even remember her name?"

He laughed dryly. "It's Jess. Give me some credit."

"And do you know anything about her?" Hailey was really pushing her luck.

"Why do you care?" Jared hopped off the counter.

"Because you're better than that."

"Because I'm better than that?" He pointed to his chest. "What about her?"

"She can do whatever she wants. I'm worried about you. You're going to be heading for a lonely life if you don't stop this."

"Glad you're worried about me, but I'd be more worried about Levi here. I think he's lost his touch."

"Shut up," I snapped at him. I was frustrated enough already, although not about the lack of sex. Strangely, that didn't bother me. But she didn't stay. I refused to believe she wasn't interested, but she was definitely making it hard.

"I'm proud of you," Hailey patted me on the shoulder.

"Great. Just what I always wanted."

"And I'm rooting for you. I like Allie and want her to stick around."

I poured myself a cup of black coffee. "She will be. Don't worry about that."

"What's your plan, Casanova?" Owen reached around me to get a mug down from the cabinet.

"I'm taking her out for lunch."

"Funny. I didn't hear you guys making plans." Owen took a seat on a stool.

"We're going out to lunch." I made my exit. I was in no mood to listen to any more crap from my friends.

Chapter Seven

I wasn't positive what her job was at the hotel, but I knew someone who would undoubtedly know. I walked into the lobby and headed right over to the desk. Luck was with me, and the manager was standing behind one of the computers.

"Good afternoon, Natalie."

The blonde woman glanced up and her posture changed immediately. She stood up straight and plastered on a smile. "Good afternoon, Levi. What a pleasant surprise."

I smiled back. "I'm actually here to see Allie. We have lunch plans."

"Oh." A look of surprise crossed her face. "I didn't know you two were friendly."

I put a hand down on the counter between us. "We're more than friendly." I don't know why I added that part. I didn't have to. Natalie was going to tell me where Allie was no matter how well I knew her.

Natalie looked torn for a second. "She's in the back."

"Thanks for the assistance." I nodded before heading back around behind the desk.

Natalie nodded. "Of course."

I walked down the narrow corridor, peeking into each cubicle and office until I saw her. She was standing by the copy machine, sorting through a pile of papers.

I quietly made my way over to her. "Ready for lunch?"

Allie's mouth fell open. "What are you doing back here, Levi?"

"Oh, Natalie told me I could come back."

"Oh, did she?" Her face scrunched up the way it seemed to always do when she was getting heated.

"Yeah. You ready?"

"I'm not having lunch with you." She lowered her voice.

I wasn't going to do the same. I raised mine. "Well, you left without letting me make you breakfast this morning, so I thought I could at least take you to lunch."

The stares of everyone around us did the trick. She took hold of my arm, and we walked down the hall.

She stopped when we were out of view and earshot of everyone else. "I don't know what kind of game you're playing, but I'm not having it."

"What game? It's just lunch." I stood right next to her, fighting the urge to pull her into my arms.

"So, you just like humiliating me in front of the people I work with?"

"That humiliated you?" I'd been going for humor not embarrassment. And, well, I also wanted to make sure any male in the vicinity knew she was completely off limits.

"Of course it did!" she hissed. "Now they think I slept with you."

"And that's a problem because…" I let a small smile slip.

"Because this is my dad's hotel. Okay, Levi? My dad's. I don't need my dad hearing about this and thinking his daughter is some sort of slut."

"Being slutty would imply spending the night with lots of guys, not just one. Heck, you can even tell him I'm your boyfriend if it makes you feel better."

"My what?"

"Your boyfriend." Isn't that what girls wanted? They wanted people to think they were in a committed relationship. I didn't care what term she used as long as I got to see her again.

"Do you even know what that word means? Have you ever had a relationship that lasted more than a few days?"

"There is a first time for everything. Most girls would want to tame me." I was pushing it, but the expression of horror on her face was worth it. Allie's reactions were too much.

"Tame you? Oh my god, leave. Just leave, okay?"

"Not until you agree to go out with me."

She wrung her hands at her sides. "You have to be kidding me."

"Not at all. I have no place to be. I'm staying here until you agree."

"Why? What angle are you playing?"

"First you accuse me of playing games and now angles. You aren't very trusting, Allison." She was going to break. She wanted to give in, and she would.

"It's Allie! And you haven't given me a reason to trust you!"

"Let me." I ignored a few employees who were watching us while trying to act like they were doing something else.

"Okay."

Okay? Nice. "Dinner tonight? I'd say lunch but I'd rather give you time to cool down."

"Don't you ever give up?"

"Never. I'm not leaving until you say yes." I needed to see her again. I needed another chance.

She sighed. "Fine. Coffee Friday night. Then you leave me alone."

"I'll pick you up at 8:00 then."

"Sure, whatever. Now leave."

"I'll miss you too." I grinned. Mission accomplished.

***

"I think I should tell her." I sipped my beer, feeling old as we sat at the unofficial Tulane bar, The Boot. We didn't go in there much anymore, but I'd had business to discuss with one of the bouncers so we decided to stay for a while.

"Tell her?" Owen looked at me like I'd lost my mind. "I hope you're kidding."

"Why not tell her? Why wait?"

"And lose her before you even get a chance?"

"Don't be so overdramatic, man. Not every guy makes girls run from him." Jared took a jab at Owen's weak spot.

Owen moved his empty beer bottle around on the table. "Most girls would run from what we are. Why would Allie be any different?"

"I have a good feeling about her." I finished off my beer. "I think she's the one."

"You've only been out with her a few times. How would you even know?" Owen eyed me warily.

"Wait. As in the one?" Jared stopped checking out the girls at the next table long enough to comment.

"I don't know for sure, but there's only one way to find out."

"How could you possibly know that from sleeping on the couch with her? You're being crazy." Jared finished his beer and pushed the empty bottle away from him.

"Just make sure you know what you're doing." Owen watched me with concern. I understood. He'd met a girl freshman year and was ready to marry her after a few months. We all told him he was crazy, but he didn't listen. He let her in on the secret that we weren't human, and she went as far as transferring schools and changing her number to get away from him. He hadn't dated anyone since.

Owen wasn't me, and Allie wasn't that stupid girl. "This is different. This is real."

"Real?" Jared snorted. "It's because she's playing hard to get. Once you bag her, the feeling will pass."

"Shut up." I pounded my hand into the table, splitting the wood. "Okay. We need to go."

I nodded an apology at the bartender as I headed for the door. He knew we'd pick up the tab later.

"This is why you have to stay away from her." Jared caught up with me outside. "She's already screwing with your brain and you haven't even fucked her."

I felt my body tense, it wanted to transform. "Use a word like bagged or fuck in reference to Allie again and I'll rip you in two."

He held up his hands in front of him. "Chill out. Just think about it. Why are you getting so bent out of shape over her? She's just a girl."

"Maybe he actually likes her. Crazy concept, I know." Owen walked ahead of us.

"Just don't lose your head over a piece of ass. It's never worth it."

I resisted the urge to punch Jared. Piece of ass? Maybe when I first met her, but she was more than that now. Jared was right about one thing, she was screwing with my brain. But that didn't mean I was going to stay away from her. It meant I was going to do the opposite.

Chapter Eight

Natalie was quick to fill me in on Allie's room number when she never showed up in the lobby. I waited around for fifteen minutes before deciding to take matters into my own hands. Allie didn't seem like the type to stand someone up.

I listened outside her door for a minute, trying to determine whether she was alone. I didn't hear anything but a loud deep sigh. I was right that something was up with her. I knocked on the door.

She swung the door open quickly like she was expecting someone. Maybe she wanted me to come up and get her. We hadn't actually discussed where I was picking her up. She wore tight gym pants and a tank top without a bra. She looked hot, but she didn't look ready for a date.

"What are you doing here?"

She was blocking the doorway, so I walked around her. There was no reason to wait out in the hall. "Did you forget we had plans?"

"Plans? Oh, yeah, coffee, I forgot." She took a seat on the couch and pulled her knees up to her chest.

I knelt down in front of her and made complete eye contact. I felt a pang in my chest as I thought about someone hurting her. "Hey, what's going on, Allie?"

"You're calling me Allie?"

"Whoa, now you're annoyed at me for calling you Allie? Can a guy ever get a break?" I tried to keep myself calm, but she didn't look like herself.

She shrugged.

"Seriously, are you okay?"

"I guess, but this summer has turned into a disaster." She exhaled loudly. "Jess left and my dad still hasn't come back. So yeah, great, I get to spend the rest of the summer all alone. Just what I needed."

I rested a hand next to her on the couch. "Hey, don't say you're alone. Don't I count for something?"

She smiled, and a weight lifted. "That's what I was looking for. It's going to be okay. But why did Jess leave?"

"It's—" She stopped suddenly. "It's personal."

My gut told me it was about Jared, but I decided to leave it. There was no reason to make her talk about something she didn't want to. "I'll take that, but on one condition."

"What?"

"Come out with me tonight. I promise I'll cheer you up."

She hesitated, and for a second I worried she'd say no. "Sure, just let me get changed."

She'd just walked into her bedroom when I heard another knock. Who else would be coming to her room? I pulled open the door, ready to defend my territory, but I quickly relaxed. It was just room service.

"Just leave it. Here you go." I handed the guy a ten, accepted the tray, and closed the door.

I opened the Styrofoam container and found a large slice of carrot cake complete with the little sugar carrot on top. "You want to eat cake first, or do you want to get changed?"

"I'm not in the mood for it anymore. You can have it or just put it in the fridge."

She disappeared into the bathroom, and I moved the cake from its container onto a plate before putting it in the fridge. I figured it would be a nice surprise for her later that night, or maybe the next morning, depending on when she came home.

I walked around the suite, noting how clean and orderly it was. Allie was either a neat freak or super organized. I was neither, but I wasn't a slob. I picked up the e-reader she must have discarded when I came in. I read a few paragraphs and it was either a romance or chic lit or something. The choice surprised me. I would have expected her to be reading something more literary.

I was about ready to turn on the TV when her cell phone rang. Curious when I saw a guy's name flash across the screen, I picked it up. "Hello?"

I heard a sound of something dropping. Allie must have heard me answer. I smiled to myself.

"Who is this? Is Allie there?" An angry male voice yelled at me from the phone.

"No, Allie's not available right now. She's getting changed." Both true statements.

"Who the hell are you?"

"Who am I? The name's Levi." I laughed to myself. This was kind of fun.

"Tell Allie Toby's on the phone. Her boyfriend Toby."

"Well, hello Toby, but I'm sorry I think Allie would have mentioned a boyfriend before she spent the night at my place. Are you sure you don't mean ex-boyfriend?" Jess had specifically said she'd sworn off men, so she definitely didn't have a boyfriend. Either this guy was delusional or he was just so hung up on her he couldn't accept she'd moved on. I heard her breathing from just inside the door. She hadn't come out to stop me. Another interesting observation.

"Go to hell, asshole."

"No, I won't go to hell, but I'll take a message." I laughed out loud this time. The call disconnected. "You can come out now. I'm off."

She opened the door slowly. "How'd you know I was listening?"

"I heard you breathing."

"You heard me through the door?" She sounded skeptical.

"You didn't really think you were fooling me, did you?" Like she couldn't hear every word I said.

"Whatever. I can't believe you answered my phone."

"You could have stopped me at any time. Something tells me you have no problem with what I told Toby." She

64

liked it. She liked that I handled the ex for her. That was a good start.

"You're right."

"I'm sure I am, but about what exactly?"

"That I don't mind what you said. He's my ex-boyfriend. We broke up a few months ago and he hasn't really accepted it."

Bingo. The situation was easy to read. "I can't say I blame him." I took her in. She'd changed into a new tank top, this time with a bra underneath, and a pair of tight dark jeans. Not quite as nice as a short skirt, but when she turned around, I decided the rear view more than made up for it.

"So, aren't we going out?" She watched me.

"Yes, the night awaits." I held open the door, and we walked out into the hallway. This was our first time going out just the two of us, and anyway you spun it, she was letting me take her out on a date.

Chapter Nine

I picked a coffee shop right down the block from the hotel. I went generic, just wanting a quiet place to sit and talk for a while. She was still bummed about her friend leaving, and I needed to change that. We'd start with coffee and then take things from there.

I led her over to an empty table. "What can I get you?"

"Oh. Just a coffee."

"Room for cream?" She didn't strike me as a black coffee kind of girl, but then again, she didn't strike me as one who read romance books either.

"Nope. I like Splenda in it though."

"Okay." I smiled before going over to the counter to get our drinks. I returned to the table with the coffees. I'd already stirred a sweetener packet in hers. She took a sip before reaching over to grab a second packet of sweetener from the plastic dish.

I watched her carefully stir the hot coffee. "Two?"

"I like things sweet."

I bet she did. The words "do you like things hard too?" swirled through my head, but I wisely kept them to myself. She might like my flirting, but that kind of comment would probably get me a slap in the face.

"What really brought you down here this summer?" I'd been trying to figure it out all week. Something wasn't adding up.

"What do you mean? Working at the hotel…"

"That's what you say, but couldn't you have gotten a job back home?" Was it all about that Toby guy? Was she running from him?

"What does it matter?"

"I'm just trying to figure you out."

"Figure me out?" She leaned forward slightly.

"You have to be the hardest girl to read."

She laughed. "I can't be that hard to read."

I laid it all out there. "We have a girl with a few months before leaving for college and instead of staying home to enjoy time with her friends, either bumming around or working some silly part time job, you drive across the country to work at a hotel for a dad who has been here all of one day since you arrived."

"Get to the point." She eyed me suspiciously.

"Either this is all an elaborate effort to get away from your ex, or you're running from something else."

She crossed her arms over her chest. "I'm not running from anything."

Defensive mannerism. I was getting close. "So it's all Toby?"

"No, it's not."

"Okay, so what is it?" Something in me needed to know. I needed to know what made this beautiful, infuriating woman tick.

"Can't there be a third choice? I wanted to try something new."

"Isn't college trying something new already?" It was definitely a big change from high school, especially if you went away from home.

"Yes, but that's different."

"Different?" I sipped my coffee.

"Yeah, I don't know, it just seemed like an adventure."

"An adventure? You're looking for an adventure, huh? Where do I sign up?" I wriggled an eyebrow at her. Now we were talking. If she wanted adventure, she'd come to the right place. Owen's warning words flooded my head, but I ignored them. This felt right. I was showing her my true self. If she wanted to run, she might as well get it over with before I fell harder. Was that possible? Was it possible to want a girl more than I already wanted her?

She laughed. "Stop. I just mean no one would ever expect me to spend a summer in New Orleans. It's different and it was so last minute. I actually quit another job at the last second so I could come here."

I feigned shock. "What? How could you?"

"Well, I guess it wasn't quitting because I didn't quite start, but I was supposed to be a lifeguard at a local beach. I changed my mind when my dad called to invite me down."

"Then I propose a toast." I lifted my cup.

"A toast? With coffee?"

"You can toast with any beverage."

"Sure, why not?" She raised her cup. "But what are we toasting?"

"To Allie's great adventure."

She laughed again as our cups touched and her eyes finally got that twinkle back. I put my cup to my lips and drank the last of my coffee like I was taking a shot. That got her smiling.

Her phone rang. I hoped it wasn't that Toby kid again.

"It's Jess. Do you mind if I get this?"

"No, not a problem." Jess I could handle. Besides, maybe if they talked, Allie would feel better about things. I wanted her in a good mood for the rest of the night.

She answered. "Hey, are you home?"

I listened in to the other end of the conversation. I couldn't catch every word, but I caught enough. "Yeah, I got in about ten minutes ago. I wanted to apologize."

"It's okay. I completely understand."

Allie glanced at the door. Another group of customers poured in. They were a rowdy bunch of tourists wearing beads they must have purchased at a store. Why people would spend money on those crappy pieces of plastic I'd never understood.

"Hey, where are you?" Jess must have heard the crowd.

"Out getting coffee." Allie smiled.

"With who?"

"Umm, can I call you later?" She looked down at the table.

Allie pushed the phone tighter against her ear. I tried to hear but the only thing I caught was my name.

She played with her coffee cup. "Maybe."

I stopped trying to listen. I'd heard what I needed to. She disconnected and sat up enough to slide her phone in her back pocket. I realized she hadn't brought a purse with her that night.

"Jess made it back?" I decided to pretend I hadn't heard the conversation for myself.

"Yeah, she just got home."

"Anything else going on?"

"Nope."

"Exciting."

She flipped her hair back. "Isn't it?"

"How's the coffee?" I made conversation but really I was planning things out in my head. If I was ready to reveal myself, I had to show her. Telling her would probably just leave her thinking I was crazy or just making it up as a joke. Showing her would be easy enough, but how was I going to handle the fall out if she didn't take it well? Should I give her some space to think about it, or force her to face it head on? I'd be willing to give her space, although I really hoped she'd shock me and accept what I was without a problem. It was a delusional thought, but I clung to it.

We talked about traveling and other random stuff for a while, and it was only a little before nine thirty when she finished her coffee. She set down her empty cup. "This was actually fun. Thanks, I needed it."

"My pleasure. See, giving me a chance wasn't so bad, was it?"

"Hey, don't read too much into it. We had coffee. End of story."

"Does it have to be the end?" I looked her straight in the eye.

"What else do you have in mind?"

"Want to meet up with my friends? I bet Hailey will come if she knows you are. I think she has a girl crush on you." Hailey had asked about her at least five times that week. She'd even texted me. That had given Jared a laugh and Owen a heart attack. He was always afraid Hailey would push me too far. I didn't care.

"A girl crush? What are you, like three?"

"No… it's just funny. She talks about you almost as much as I do." Had I said that out loud? I guess telling her I talked about her wasn't necessarily a bad thing. She already knew how I felt.

"I think she's pretty cool too. Definitely different from my other friends."

"Different is good, right?" If she liked different, I might be okay.

"It can be."

"Are you up for hanging out more?" I asked it as a question, but I wasn't taking no for an answer. Now that I'd built up the anticipation, I couldn't back down.

"Yeah, okay."

I led her through the French Quarter, watching her reaction to everything. She might be used to city life, but

New Orleans was something altogether different. Although touristy, the Quarter was still a special place, and I was glad she seemed interested in it. If things were going to work between us, she'd have to start calling New Orleans home. Leaving wasn't an option for me. I was crown prince, and the throne was in the basement of the Crescent City Hotel.

She stopped short in front of a dark bar on the corner. I smiled when I saw what got her attention.

"Wow, are those people seriously dressed up as vampires?" Her eyes were glued on a couple of humans who were holding up a chalice and pretending to drink blood.

I laughed. "If you think those people are weird, you'd be freaked out by the real thing."

"The real thing? Very funny." She started walking again.

"What, you don't think vampires are real?" Here it was. How much did she believe in the legends already?

"No, and I'm glad they aren't."

"Why? Do they scare you?" I stopped and took her arm so I could turn her to look at me.

"Does the thought of blood sucking monsters scare me? Hell yes. Who wouldn't be scared of that?"

I laughed again. Allie was in for one hell of a surprise. "Trust me, sweetheart, in New Orleans, vampires are the least of your worries."

"What do you mean?"

"I'm really glad you asked that."

Her face paled slightly. "What are you talking about?"

"You'll have to wait and see."

"Okay, listen, scaring me isn't a good way to get me interested, so if you have any weird tricks up your sleeve. just shelve them." She balled her hands into fists. I could tell it wasn't anger, but nerves that prompted the action.

"No tricks, hon." I pulled out my phone and texted Owen. It was still early, but I hoped they'd made it downtown already. The plan was to meet them on my own if things didn't go anywhere with Allie and to bring her if they did. The part of the plan they didn't know yet was that I wasn't waiting.

You there yet?

Yeah. Hailey tagged along too. Is it just you?

No. We're both coming.

Cool.

I'm doing it. There, I'd said it.

You're crazy.

Don't act surprised.

I pocketed my phone. "We're meeting everyone over at Club 360."

"What's that?"

"The lounge on the top of the World Trade Center down by the river."

"Okay, is it a cool view?"

"Yeah, it's got a good view." I laughed again. She had no idea how good of a view she was about to see.

"You promise you aren't luring me into some trap?"

"A trap? No. Let's just call it a new experience." The first wave of nerves hit me. Was I really doing this? Was I really taking the chance? Yes. There was no backing down.

We walked in a comfortable silence, and I held open the door when we arrived. There was a short wait for an elevator, but it was empty when we stepped in. I watched her, trying to hide my nerves.

The elevator doors opened on the top floor, dumping us out right at the club. I led her through the crowd, noticing that she kept checking out her outfit.

"Don't worry, we won't be here long." Not that she had to care about being underdressed.

"Why are we here at all then?"

"Do you ever stop asking questions?" To handle my nerves, I decided to give her a hard time. That usually worked for both of us.

"I only ask this many questions when I fear for my well-being."

"I assure you that you are in good hands." I put an arm around her waist, needing her close to me. Her touch reminded me of how important this was. I needed her to know what I really was. She had to accept I wasn't human, and hopefully she'd like the perks that came with it. I had more to offer her than she could imagine. I spotted my friends. "I see them."

The three of them were seated at a small window table. Only Jared had a drink. Owen and Hailey were looking around the room nervously.

"Allie! I'm so glad you came!" Hailey jumped out of her seat and hugged her. Allie beamed. It seems that the girl crush went both ways.

Allie smoothed out her tank top, bringing my attention to her stomach. I was sure it was toned and smooth. Picturing her skin helped relax me. "Yeah, I needed a night out."

"Where's your friend?" Jared asked casually.

"My friend? You mean Jess? She's back in New York, thanks to you."

I was right. It was about Jared.

Jared gave me a confused look. "She left? What does that have to do with me?"

"Nothing. Forget I said anything." Allie slipped into the empty seat next to Hailey.

"Okay..." Jared shrugged.

She gazed out the window, and once again, I wanted to know what she was thinking. Was she still upset about Jess? Was she just enjoying the view? The only view I cared about was her.

My friends watched me carefully. They were trying to see if I was going to chicken out. I still could. I could just ask Allie to dance and then take her home. Theoretically, I could just do it another night, but I wasn't a quitter. Just like I wasn't giving up on getting her, I wasn't backing down on my plans. Hailey asked me the silent question, and I nodded.

"All right, are you guys ready to go?" Hailey asked.

Allie turned away from the window. "What, already? I haven't even had a chance to enjoy the view."

I leaned over close to her. "You think this is a good view? Oh, just you wait."

"What are you talking about?"

"You sure about this, Levi? You know there is no turning back, right?" Owen looked at me, trying to avoid catching Allie's eye.

"Absolutely." I smiled.

Jared pushed out his chair. "Well, then, let's get going. It's supposed to rain later tonight."

"Why does the rain matter?" Allie's face appeared to be a mix of nerves and excitement. I really hoped the excitement won over.

"Are you ready to find out just how far the rabbit hole goes, sweetheart?" I reached out a hand to her. She needed to come with me willingly.

"Rabbit hole?" She seemed to hesitate. "Umm, sure?"

She put her hand in my mine. I led her through the crowd, and past the elevators. Jared took the lead, and we walked into the stairwell. She turned to look at me once more before starting up the stairs.

We were about halfway up when she finally questioned our destination. "Okay, why are we going to the roof?"

She was frightened, and I wanted to fix everything for her. The problem was I couldn't give her any easy answers. "No more questions." I tried to calm both of us.

"But—"

I gently pressed the palm of my hand into her back, hoping it had an effect on her. Touching her in anyway set me simultaneously on fire and put me at ease. "No more questions."

"It's all right. We're not taking you up there to kill you." Hailey laughed. Great. Because that didn't sound creepy.

Allie let out a deep breath. "Fine."

We walked up the remaining stairs and into the muggy night. The lights of the city reflected off the water. This was it. No turning back. I used her moment of distraction to pull off my shirt. My friends did the same. Hailey pulled off her sweater so she was just in a tank top.

I moved behind Allie and wrapped my arms around her waist.

She struggled against me so I loosened my hold. I let out a slow deep breath.

"What the hell..." she trailed off as she backed away from me. Her eyes widened.

I tried to keep my voice as soothing as possible. "Now don't freak out. I promised you I wouldn't hurt you, and I always keep my promises."

"Are you guys in a cult or something? Because if you are, I'm really not interested. I won't tell anyone anything, but if you don't mind, I'm leaving." She crossed her arms protectively.

"Chill out!" Jared yelled as his eyes changed to black. He was already transforming. He was the one who needed to stay calm.

I glared at him. "Don't talk to her like that."

He nodded, understanding the warning in my command. His eyes slowly returned to normal.

Hailey took a few steps toward Allie. I let her. Maybe a female would put her more at ease. "We're not a cult. It's more like a very special society." That was probably a good way to put it.

"A special society?" Allie's thoughts were clear on her face. She thought we were high or psychotic.

"Maybe it would be better if we just showed her." Owen smiled at her, and I appreciated him trying to help even though I knew he didn't support my decision. "You were sure you wanted this Levi, so there is no turning back."

He walked over to the edge of the building and raised a hand in a small wave before taking a backwards step and disappearing from sight.

"Oh my god! What the hell? Did he just kill himself?" Allie started shaking and crying. I wanted to reach out for her, but I wanted to let everyone go first.

"Owen's fine," Hailey said before jumping off with Jared right behind her.

Allie closed her eyes. I moved behind her again and wrapped her up in my arms. Her warm body fit perfectly against my bare chest.

"You said you wanted an adventure." I tightened my hold.

I let myself transform, reveling in the familiar feel of my large black wings extending from my back. I felt a wave of strength roll over me as I prepared to jump. I'd never flown with someone in my arms before, and Allie wasn't just anyone. She was everyone.

I stepped off.

I could tell she still had her eyes closed. Her body was so tense. She needed to see that everything was going to be okay. "Open your eyes," I whispered.

She let out the tiniest start of a scream before going silent. I continued our decent and then leveled us out just above the water. Part one was over. If she accepted me, wings and all, I may have found my mate. If she didn't, I wasn't sure what I was going to do. In the deepest part of my heart and soul, I knew there was no one else for me.

Forever

a crescent chronicles novella

Chapter One

Flying with Allie in my arms was a whole new experience. Her closeness set off something inside me that made the usual rush from flying so much better. I let myself enjoy the flight, pushing aside any lingering doubt over how she'd react. If this was going to be my only flight with her, I was going to enjoy it. But it couldn't be the only one. There was no way I could let her go.

Eventually I landed. Putting off the inevitable wouldn't help. She seemed to be handling herself well, but there was no reason to push my luck any more than necessary.

I set her down, and she stumbled away from me. Her quick movement surprised me, and she fell down onto the grass. She clutched the green strands for dear life. I thought back on my first flight. It was different for me. Flying was like breathing. I tried to put myself in her shoes. She must have been terrified.

She stared up at me through her long, damp eyelashes. "What the hell are you? Oh-my-god you're angels, aren't you? I'm dead. I'm actually dead?"

I laughed. "Do you really think I'm an angel?" I was used to the comparison. With long black wings, people had gotten us confused on many occasions.

"A fallen angel?" She asked, looking around at all four of us.

I laughed lightly, hoping to put her at ease, but I was determined that she see me for who I really was. "We're not angels of any sort." I stepped toward her.

"Then what are you?" She scooted away from me, and my chest clenched. Was she afraid of me? She squeezed her eyes shut.

"Open your eyes, sweetheart." I kneeled down and placed my hands on her trembling shoulders. "Open your eyes."

"No, this has to be some messed up dream."

"It's not a dream." I kept my voice low, soft. I needed to put her at ease.

"Yes, it is."

"No, it's not. Accept it already," Jared snapped at her. I glared at him. If he screwed this up for me he was a goner.

She looked ready to snap back, but then she pressed her lips together and paused for a moment before turning her eyes to me. "If this isn't a dream, then what are you? What's going on?"

"We're Pterons," Hailey said gently.

"Pterons?" Allie asked, repeating the word carefully as though she were trying it out.

"We're shifters, Allie," I tried to stay gentle and calm. I needed to put her at ease. One slip up and she might run.

"Shifters? Like what, a werewolf?"

Jared laughed. "We're not like werewolves. That's like saying humans are like chimps."

"Humans? Wait, because you guys aren't human…" Her gorgeous green eyes widened with a mix of shock and fear.

"Like I said, we're shifters. At one time our people shifted into crows, but over time we became more of a hybrid. It's more efficient." I simplified the explanation as much as possible.

"Like natural selection or something?" she asked absently. She was staring off in the distance. I hoped she wasn't in shock.

"Something like that." I picked up her hands. "You okay?"

"I'm not sure."

"It really doesn't change anything." Hailey took a few steps closer to us.

"You're standing there with giant wings coming out of your back, yet you tell me that nothing has changed?"

"What she means is that we're still the same people you wanted to hang out with in the beginning of the night, just *enhanced*," Owen said with a small smile.

"Enhanced? So other than flying, what can you do?"

"Other than flying?" I couldn't help but laugh—not at her, but at the idea. "Yes, because flying is so commonplace. But to answer your question we have some other skills, but I think this is enough for tonight."

"Oh." She closed her mouth as though she couldn't possibly say anything else.

"You're funny, you know that?" I tried to help her to her feet, but she pulled away from me. I tried not to let the physical rejection worry me.

"Umm, can you put those things away?"

"Those *things*? Our wings? Yes, we can put them away." If it was just the wings freaking her out I could take care of it. I retracted them.

"Turn around." She stood up and took a step toward me.

I turned and reveled in the feel of her hands on the ridges of my back. She wouldn't be able to see much in the faint moonlight, but the spot was sensitive, and her touch sent a thrill through me. My mind flashed to an image of having her in my bed while in my true form.

"Are you done manhandling Levi yet, or are we going to stay here all night?"

"Shut up, Jared," Hailey snapped.

"She can manhandle me all she wants." I reluctantly turned back. I wanted her hands on me all night. "You ready to go home or do you want to see more?"

She crossed her arms over her chest. "I'm ready to go home." I didn't miss the resoluteness in her tone. She wanted me to know she wasn't playing around.

"We'll see you tomorrow, right?" Hailey asked. Her voice waivered, and I realized she cared about Allie's response nearly as much as I did.

"Yeah, sure," she said without much conviction. Hailey and Owen exchanged a look.

"All right, if you're sure." I wrapped my arms around her. At least I'd get another flight with Allie.

"Wait, stop!" She struggled in my arms, and I quickly released her.

She turned to look at me. "I never said I wanted to fly again. How far are we from the hotel?"

"Oh, right. We can get a cab." I tried to hide the disappointment in my voice. I wanted to hold her body against mine, to take her to a place that no human ever could.

"No. I can get a cab. Where are we?"

"We're at the levee. You sure you don't want me to take you home? At least let me walk you to the street."

She seemed to mull it over for a second. "All right, fair enough."

That was something. I nodded at Hailey, signaling for her to call a cab before I followed Allie down to the road.

The cab pulled up, and everything about the moment felt wrong. She wasn't supposed to be leaving alone. She was supposed to be going home with me, but she needed time. I needed to at least give her the night.

"Good night," I said quietly as I watched her slip into the cab.

My heart soared slightly when she smiled just as the cab pulled away. The smile wasn't much, but I was taking it. I still had a chance, and I was going to use it to its fullest.

Chapter Two

"So that went well." Jared patted my back after Allie's cab disappeared around the corner.

"Shut up."

"I mean at least she didn't run screaming like Owen's girl did... or wait, she still could."

Owen ignored Jared's rib. "She was overwhelmed, but that isn't necessarily a bad thing. Maybe she just needs time to let it settle."

"She's going to stay." Hailey said it quietly. I wasn't used to Hailey ever being quiet, and I wasn't sure if the change was a good or bad thing.

"You think so?" I turned to Hailey, needing any encouragement I could get.

"Yes. It's the way she looked at you. She was scared, but curious. She really likes you. I think you've at least got a chance."

"Just don't fuck it up." Jared laughed.

"I'm not going to." I paced around trying to figure out what my next step was going to be. "I need to see her."

"Oh no. None of that." Hailey shook her head emphatically.

"I'm just going to look."

"You do realize you sound like a certified stalker, right? 'Just going to look'?" Hailey didn't hide her opinion on the matter.

"I need to make sure she's okay. This was a lot to take in."

Hailey rolled her eyes. "That doesn't excuse you invading her privacy."

"It's not like I'm going to try to see her naked." Although I hoped she'd very knowingly give me that opportunity soon.

"I can't be part of this." She gritted her teeth. "But I like Allie, so I can't walk away either."

"You can look first, make sure she's appropriately attired."

She groaned. "I'm doing this for Allie and not you. Remember that."

"Do it for whatever reason you want."

"Let's get this over with. I'm not letting you watch her while she's sleeping."

I smiled. "I wasn't planning to wait."

We flew over to the hotel and landed in the shadows covering much of the courtyard.

I waited impatiently. "Ok, go first. I'm ready when you are."

Hailey flew up to Allie's balcony, and I waited impatiently. Jared and Owen wisely stayed quiet. I didn't care what their opinion was.

Hailey landed next to me. "She's dressed."

I flew up and landed, being extra careful to stay hidden as I looked in the balcony window. She was just turning off the lights and sipping a glass of what appeared to be water.

Allie was okay, and for the night that was all I needed to know. I reluctantly left my perch.

"Feeling better, stalker?" Hailey glared. I felt a tinge of guilt at invading Allie's privacy and making Hailey help.

"Yes. We can go."

"You have it bad." Hailey nudged me with her arm.

I didn't respond. I'd never hear the end of it from my friends.

***

I wasn't sure what time Allie usually got up, but to play it safe I showed up at the hotel around nine. After the night she'd had, I doubted she'd be getting up earlier. I heard her moving around in her room, so I pulled out my phone and found some games to mess around with. If last night had been stalking, what was this? I left the floor a few times when I heard other guests getting ready to leave their rooms, but I was back outside her room leaning against the wall when finally, two hours later, her door opened. She walked out gripping her phone in her hand.

"Hoping for a call from someone?"

She noticed me and her face broke into a bright smile. My heart soared.

"How long have you been out here?"

"Awhile." I straightened and took a step toward her. The smile had been the only invitation I needed.

"Oh. You could have knocked…" she trailed off. Her eyes were locked on my face.

"I figured there was no need to push you anymore than I did last night. But I had to see you—to see if you were still reacting well." I spoke carefully. She seemed happy to see me, but that didn't mean she wasn't afraid.

"Why wouldn't I be reacting well?" She smiled. I had to love that sense of humor.

"It's not every day that you see something like that. Maybe in my life, but not yours."

"I guess it would be normal in yours."

I returned her smile. "Any chance I can take you to a late breakfast?"

"That depends. How are we getting there?" She touched her neck, and I got the feeling she wasn't asking out of fear.

I laughed, still trying to put her at ease. "We're walking, but would you want to fly with me again?"

"I could be persuaded."

I ran a hand down her cheek. Her skin was so soft. "I'm glad. There's more I want to show you."

"So are we going to go now or—"

As much as I wanted to take her flying again, I knew I couldn't. "Uh, it's broad daylight, Al. Don't you think someone would notice?"

"Oh, you only fly at night? And now you're calling me Al?"

"We usually only fly at night, but there are exceptions I'm not getting into right now. And I am still trying to settle on what name I like best."

"Doesn't my opinion count?"

I moved closer to her, edging her back against the wall. "Your opinion always counts, but I already told you I'm not calling you what everyone else does. I'm going to have my own name for you."

"What, like you name a pet? That sounds kind of possessive."

"It is kind of possessive, Al." I winked and took her hand. "Have you been to Café du Monde yet?"

She shook her head.

"Good, let's go." I held onto her hand and led her to the elevator. The thought of introducing Allie to something quintessentially New Orleans had me excited. I loved my city, and if I had any hope of keeping Allie around past the summer, I needed to make her love it too.

I watched her the whole way down on the elevator. I was vaguely aware of other people entering, but no one else mattered. The only thing worth focusing on was her.

One of the bellboys was at the front entrance when we walked down. He smiled at Allie, and I choked down my annoyance. She was holding my hand not his. "Hey Allie,

I haven't seen you or Jess today, where have you been hiding?"

"Jess went back to New York," she sounded sad. I knew she missed her friend, and I was going to have to help her get over it.

"Oh. She really left? Did you ever find out what was going on with her?" The kid didn't bother to hide the disappointment in his voice. I felt relief myself. He wasn't into Allie.

"Personal reasons." She shrugged, revealing a tension in her shoulders I was dying to fix. "I'll see you around."

I nodded stiffly to the kid as we walked outside into the bright sunlight.

I took her through Jackson Square, watching as she took in all the art hung up on the wrought iron fence. She paused as we passed St. Louis Cathedral. She seemed to appreciate the architecture as much as I did. "There's nothing quite like New Orleans, huh?"

"Not really. I mean it has a similar feel to Paris, but it definitely has a flavor all of its own." There was something in her expression that made me wonder whose flavor she was talking about. Her eyes took me in—she was checking me out, and I definitely enjoyed the attention. The only thing that would have made it better would have been her hands doing what her eyes were.

I forced myself to stop daydreaming about her hands on me. "You still interested in breakfast?"

"Absolutely." She held my gaze. I'd never met a girl who could manage that for long.

After slipping under the green and white awning of Café Du Monde, I pulled out her chair. Once she was seated, I sat down across from her. The table was small enough that my legs brushed against hers with my slightest movements. I didn't mind at all, and I sensed she didn't either.

As soon as the server walked over I asked for two orders of beignets and two chicory coffees. I wondered if Allie had ever had the flavorful coffee before.

The coffee came out first, followed by still hot beignets. Allie looked adorable as she spilled powdered sugar all over herself. The best part was instead of getting embarrassed she just laughed. I'd never met a girl with such genuine confidence. It wasn't an act, it was who she was.

"Wow, these are good!"

"What isn't there to like about fried dough covered in sugar?" I resisted the urge to wipe some powdered sugar off her face. I refused to do anything that would mess with the confident, happy smile on her face. "So, Princeton, huh?"

"Yup. Home of the Tigers."

I nearly choked on my coffee. She had this quirky sarcastic sense of humor that took me by surprise sometimes. "Yeah, because that's what comes to mind first when someone says Princeton."

"What comes to mind for you?"

"Oh, I don't know. How about uptight preps who wouldn't know how to have a good time if it bit them on the ass?" I leaned back in my chair.

"Ouch. You don't think I know how to have fun?"

"On the contrary hon, I know you can have fun. It's the others I'm worried about. I'm afraid that next time I see you you'll be a walking Ralph Lauren ad." Pushing Allie's buttons had become one of my favorite pastimes. Without fail it made those cheeks of hers turn pink, and she got this sexy gleam in her eyes.

"What makes you think you'll ever see me after this summer?"

"You've had your taste Al. Even if you leave in August, you'll be back for more." I'd make sure of it.

"And what are you referring to exactly?"

"The city." I paused. "Of course."

"Of course. If you're done, it's my turn."

"Your turn for what?" I asked with genuine curiosity.

"To ask a question."

"I wasn't aware we were taking turns."

She ignored me. "So, you're graduating this year, right?"

I nodded, waiting to see where she was going with the line of questioning.

"What's next for you?"

"Uh, taking over the family business." I looked away. As much as I'd shared the night before, I wasn't ready to reveal everything. That might make her run away faster.

"Which is?"

"You asked your question." She did say we were taking turns.

"Whoa, are there more secrets?"

"It's kind of hard to explain. Let's just say it's a leadership position." That was true—although it wasn't the kind of leadership position she was probably thinking.

"You're not going to elaborate?"

"My turn." I turned the conversation on her. There was so much more to learn about her.

"Fine."

"So, what's the story with Toby?" I wasn't going to waste my question.

"What do you mean? I already told you he's my ex."

"Yeah, but why is he your ex?"

"Why do you even care?"

"Eh, just curiosity." I knew he was a big part of why she was in New Orleans. I wanted to know more.

"And why would I indulge that curiosity when you evaded my question?"

"My good looks?" I took a long sip of my coffee. I'd been so content watching her that I'd barely had any yet.

"Very funny. Really there isn't much to tell. We dated about a year, and we worked, but I got tired of the lack of sparks. I brought up my concerns and he brushed them off, so I broke up with him." She was holding back. I knew it but decided not to press the issue. I was more concerned with what she had said.

"Lack of sparks? You're looking for passion then?"

A slight tinge of pink crossed her cheeks. Had I finally made Allie blush?

"Okay, my turn again. What's with Jared and Owen?"

"What do you mean?" I tried to predict where she was going with the question. She already knew they weren't human, what else would she want to know about?

"You act like girls or something. You're never apart."

Like girls? Not exactly. "They're not here now."

"I get this vibe that they answer to you or something. Does this have to do with the 'family business'?"

Perceptive. "Maybe."

"Seriously? You're evading my question again?"

"And here I thought girls liked a man of mystery."

She groaned. "On that note, are you ready to get going?"

"Sure." I tossed some cash down on the table.

She stopped to dust some powdered sugar off her skirt. She needed to wear skirts all the time. I'd never seen a better pair of legs. "So, where to now?"

I forced my eyes up to her face. "Where do you want to go?"

"Hmm, I don't know."

"What would you be doing if you were home?" Today needed to be about her. Or at least about making her comfortable.

"I'd probably be at the beach." Her face brightened. "It's pretty much my favorite place to be."

"I'll have to keep that in mind. The beach is a little hard to give you right now, but how about we check out the French Market?"

"Shopping?"

"Is that a problem?"

"Not at all, I am just surprised by the suggestion." Her arm brushed against mine as we walked.

"It's not like I'm taking you to the mall."

"True, but you don't seem like the shopping type."

"If you're done complaining…" I gave her a slight smile.

"Lead the way." She gestured with her hands. She was cute that way.

Allie let out a sigh of relief as we entered the French Market. Aside from my desire to show her more of the classic New Orleans downtown, I knew she'd appreciate the shade. Even after twenty-two years in New Orleans, I still wasn't always prepared for the brutally hot and humid summers. I'm sure coming from the north it was nearly oppressive.

I led her carefully through the crowds, mentally cursing myself for suggesting the stop. Shade or not, it wasn't worth dealing with so many tourists. "I think I remember now why I don't come here much."

"Not one for crowds?" she asked.

"Not really. You?"

"I actually kind of like them. I think it's why I like New York City so much. I love the feeling of getting lost in a big crowd."

"I learn something new about you every day." I guided her down the center aisle. I knew she was a city girl, but I didn't realize quite how much she liked it.

"I think you won that contest last night." She smiled once again surprising me with how well she was taking things. I kept waiting for it to be too much for her. "Well, we can leave if you want."

"Not until we do one thing."

"Okay..."

"You like sweets, right?" I asked. Her answer was important. If a girl liked sweets, providing dessert was a crucial part of a date.

"Of course."

"Loretta's has some great pralines you've got to try."

I stepped into the small store. She hung back, so I hurried with my selections. I was glad she trusted me to pick hers out. I went with the traditional. Some things are just better classic.

She took a small bite and smiled. Evidently I'd picked well.

"Ready?" I took her hand again, loving the feel of her small hand in my own.

We walked back through Jackson Square and directly over to the next stop of our day. The large building didn't look like much on the outside, but it was the roof I wanted her to see. "The view here isn't quite as good as last night, but it's pretty nice."

"Pat O's?" She pointed to the wooden sign.

"It's Pat O's on the River, good drinks and a nice view."

"Drinks in the middle of the afternoon?"

"You're in N'awlins Al, get used to it." I led her inside and into the elevator. We took it right up, and we walked through the indoor bar directly out onto the patio.

We passed a waitress on our way out. "Hi Levi."

I gave her a curt nod. Had I met the woman before? I didn't know and didn't care. The only girl on my mind was currently holding my hand.

We took seats at a high top table overlooking the river. It was easy to forget that New Orleans was a seaport city in day to day life, but one glance at the river reminded you of the rich history and significance of the Crescent City. I wasn't exactly a history buff, but I loved my city.

"You weren't kidding. This is a great view." She glanced up at the awning. She seemed grateful for the shade from the intense heat.

"I thought you would like it. You seem to really like good views."

"The usual?" A waiter interrupted.

"Yes, and a hurricane for her."

"All right, be right out with those." The waiter quickly hurried off.

"Does everyone who works here know you?" she leaned forward slightly in her chair.

"Not *everyone*." Admittedly almost all of the employees did at least know of me.

"Well anyway, what did you order me?"

"You'll like it. It's pretty much the signature drink of the city and the specialty drink here, so you need to have it at least once."

"Is it as good as the other drink you keep buying me?"

"Maybe not as good, but you'll still enjoy it."

"What did you get?"

"Whiskey."

"How do you know I wouldn't prefer that?" There was a challenge in her words.

"I don't take you as the type to take your liquor straight." I watched her, daring her to contradict me. I knew her well enough already to know what she'd want to drink.

"You're right. I was just asking."

The waiter brought over our drinks, and Allie took a slow sip. She smiled and closed her eyes for a moment. "Ah, it's such a gorgeous afternoon."

"I'm glad to see you enjoying yourself."

"Is there any chance you'll take me—" The blare of a barge drowned her out. "Any chance you'll—" The barge blared again.

"What were you asking?"

"Any chance of a repeat performance of last night?"

"You liked that, huh?" I teased.

"Yeah, I can't say I've ever had a ride like that before."

A middle-aged woman at the table next to us coughed, and I decided to run with the innuendo. "Sure baby, I'll take you for a ride anytime."

Allie hit my leg under the table, and I pretended it hurt. "Ouch."

"You so deserved that."

"You're the one that wants the ride." I unsuccessfully tried to stifle a laugh.

"Is that a yes? You'll take me again?"

"Of course, I have no intentions of letting you down."

Chapter Three

Bringing Allie back to my place for the second time was a different experience. This visit wasn't to try to talk her into staying the night; it was about getting her used to my world little by little.

When I opened the front door, I wasn't surprised to find Jared and Owen playing video games. They barely acknowledged us when we walked in. I didn't mind.

"Can I get you anything?" I noticed Allie eyeing my black and white photography of New Orleans street scenes on the wall. Maybe that was another interest we shared.

"I'm fine, but thanks." She was nervous. Not overly so, but being in my home put her on edge. I needed to change that because if I had my way she'd be spending a lot of time there.

"Want a tour?"

"A tour? Is there really that much more to see?"

"Of course there is. You never even saw my room last time." I headed off down the hall to my room assuming she'd follow.

"You probably remember that's Jared's room," I pointed, not wanting to bring up the sore subject of Jess more than I had to. "Owen's is over there and I'm here on the end." I walked into my room, excited at the thought of her finally entering it.

"Wow, you don't see too many beds that big in college apartments."

"How many college apartments have you been in? Didn't you just graduate high school?" Once again I had to tease her.

"I have older friends…"

"Older friends who like to show you their bedrooms with inadequately sized beds? Good to know."

She glanced around at my room. By the expression on her face I probably should have cleaned up before inviting her in, but it really wasn't that bad. You could actually see the hardwood floor.

"So is it Owen who keeps the rest of this place clean? I mean, obviously it's not you."

"You automatically assume it's Owen?"

"Yeah… wait, don't tell me it's Jared."

"Okay, I won't."

"Wow, Jared the neat freak," she said with surprise.

"You're not his biggest fan, are you?"

"No, not at all." She could be so honest. It was both refreshing and terrifying.

"It has something to do with your friend, doesn't it?"

A frown marred her face, and I immediately regretted my line of questioning. "I don't want to talk about Jess, okay?"

"Sure, but Jared's not all bad."

"If you say so."

"I do. He's had my back since we were kids, and I think he kind of grows on you." I decided to change the subject. "Do you still want to fly?"

"Yes!" She got giddy. This girl was incredible.

"All right, let me talk to the guys. I'll be right back."

She was sitting on the edge of my bed when I returned. All I wanted to do was push her down on my bed and kiss every last inch of her body. I refrained. It wasn't the right time. "All right, they're in. Owen's going to call Hailey and have her meet us."

"Where are we going exactly?"

"It's a surprise."

"What if I don't like surprises?" She asked.

"Come on, Al, you like surprises." I leaned over, placing a hand on either side of her on the bed.

"What makes you say that?"

"I just know." I kissed her lightly, forcing myself to break the kiss before it could get heated. By the look on her face I'd left her wanting more. Perfect.

I pulled off my t-shirt and grabbed a hoodie sweatshirt for her. "First I can't get you into my room, and now I can't get you out of it?"

"Shut up." She followed me into the hallway.

Owen and Jared were waiting for us by the open front door.

"Put this on." I tossed her the sweatshirt so she wouldn't get cold.

"You want me to wear something that was in a ball on the floor?"

"It's clean. I just did laundry." Clearly the girl was the neat freak type. I'd have to work on that.

"So why was it on the floor?"

Owen laughed.

"Just put it on. We're not going high, but it's a longer flight and it's going to be cold."

She shook her head. "No thanks."

"Fine, suit yourself. But at least bring it with you. You'll thank me when you're freezing later." Hopefully I'd get the chance to warm her up.

"Somehow I doubt that, but I'll bring it."

"All right, you ready?" If she was going to be stubborn there was nothing I could do.

"Definitely." Her whole face glowed.

I laughed. Her excitement had me amped up as well. "Wow, you really are pumped up for this."

"Why? Do most girls not react this way?"

"Most girls? How many girls do you think I've flown before?"

"I'd assume quite a few." There was a jealous tone to her voice I didn't mind.

"Naw, Allie, you're his first. Isn't that sweet? Okay, end of story, let's go," Jared said impatiently.

"Seriously? Then why'd you take me?" Her eyes widened.

"It felt right. Let's get out of here." I wasn't ready to tell her just how special she was to me. First, I needed to show her just how impossible it would be for her to resist me. "Oh, you might want to hold those flip-flops."

She enfolded her flip-flops in the sweatshirt after following us outside. I hoped the second flight didn't disappoint.

I wrapped my arms around her waist. Once again her body fit perfectly. "Have fun."

I purposely flew low enough to keep the skyline in view. I wanted her to have the real experience. I held her tight, hoping she knew just how securely I had her.

The lights of the city disappeared as the ocean came into view. I fell back, wanting to give her more time to enjoy herself. Her body was relaxed, but I could nearly feel the excitement flowing through her. This was a girl who was born to fly. She was born to be with me.

I flew along the shore until her shivering outweighed her excitement. I landed gently on the sand.

I set her down carefully, and she immediately began trying to warm up her arms. I wanted to take over that job myself, but I held back and just smiled. Her body language would let on if she wanted my help.

"Why don't you get cold when you fly?" Her eyes lingered on my bare chest.

"My body's designed for it, yours isn't." But her body was designed for me.

"Oh, I guess that makes sense." She took in a deep breath and buried her toes in the sand. "I can't believe you brought me to a beach."

"You like it?"

"I love it. But where are we?"

"Grand Isle."

"I've never heard of it, but it's nice to know there's a beach so close."

I led her over to join my friends.

Hailey added kindling to a roaring bonfire. "I'm so glad you weren't scared away." She gave Allie a friendly smile.

"Me too." Allie craned her neck to watch the stars.

"Be honest, you love it." I slipped an arm around her waist. "You're the one who asked me to take you flying again."

"Nice, it's pretty cool right?" Hailey's face lit up. She really cared about Allie, and I knew she'd be an important ally.

"Very. It's, uh, definitely different, but I like different."

I hoped she kept that attitude.

***

We sat by the fire for an hour or so. I enjoyed the feeling of her body snuggled right next to mine, but I needed some time alone with her. I leaned in to whisper in her ear, "Want to take a walk?"

"Sounds good." She stood immediately and waved to Hailey.

We walked off into the darkness, and I held her hand firmly in my own. I'd never been a big hand holder, but it's like I needed to have hers in mine. I needed to touch her constantly, and I wanted her to know she was always safe with me—even if I was far from safe to most anyone else.

She tugged on my hand, and I gladly followed her down closer to the water.

She took in another deep breath. "There is nothing like the beach at night."

"You like it at night, too? I was worried you wouldn't like it without the sun." I wondered if I was unique in craving the quiet shadows of the dark beach.

"I like the beach during the day, but I love it at night. There is just something about listening to the waves in the darkness and the soft glow of the stars reflecting off the water."

"Yeah. It's nice." I moved behind her, and she leaned into me. We stood that way for several minutes before I turned her to look at me.

She looked like a dream standing there in the glimmering of the moonlight. I studied her face, looking for a sign that she was something more than the beautiful human that had attracted me from the moment we met. Every part of me knew how significant she was to me, but I wanted more proof. "You're so beautiful. So unbelievably beautiful…" I trailed off as my lips gave in to what they had wanted to do all day.

I started the kiss off gentle, but it didn't stay that way for long. The second she responded I deepened the kiss, not bothering to hold back like I had at the bar. I tightened my arms around her while my tongue explored every corner of her mouth.

She let out a moan, and I lowered her down into the sand.

The sand was damp below us, but neither of us cared, all that mattered was our closeness. My doubts were gone. It was her. After all those years, I'd found her.

I tried to control myself. I struggled to calm myself down when all I wanted to do was have her completely. Instead I kept the pace slow, satisfying my need to touch her body by tracing my fingers over her stomach. I pushed up the bottom of her tank top, eagerly exposing more of her lightly sun kissed skin. Her body was so responsive. She enjoyed my touch as much as I enjoyed hers, and I kept my body above hers, cutting out the wind.

She closed her eyes, moaning again as she ran her fingers down my back. She paused on the nearly invisible lines that served as the only clue to what I really was. She moved her fingers lower, and I groaned. Her cool hands felt so good on my warm skin.

I needed to see more of her. I shifted her so I could pull off her tank top. I marveled at the tops of her breasts peeking out over her light pink bra.

I trailed kisses from her ear down to her neck. I started to slip one of her bra straps down her shoulder, ready to expose more of her body to me.

I heard footsteps but ignored them. It was just Hailey, and I didn't care. I needed Allie, and Hailey was just going to have to wait.

Unfortunately she didn't turn away before interrupting our moment. "Are you guys ever coming back? Oh wow, leaving now," she stammered.

Allie sat up, quickly covering her chest with her arms. I choked down my groan, but it was going to take a moment to calm the rest of my body. I would have another chance. She'd been so responsive, her eyes so full of longing. This wasn't the end. It was just the beginning.

"Wait, no Hailey. It's not what you think." Allie pulled on her tank top and stood up. She turned to look at me.

I was still working to calm myself as I waited on the sand. "If it wasn't what she thought, then what was it?"

"Almost a mistake," she mumbled before hurrying after Hailey.

I didn't let her words get to me. Her true feelings were the ones she'd been showing me before we were interrupted. "It didn't seem like you were worried about that a minute ago!"

She didn't answer.

I listened in on her conversation with Hailey. I wondered when Allie would realize just how well I could hear.

"I'm really sorry you had to see that."

Hailey smiled at her. "You don't have to explain. I actually think it's kind of cute."

"Cute?"

"Yeah... I don't know, I think you guys work together..." Hailey trailed off as I caught up with them, and we walked the remaining distance to the fire.

"Nice of you two to join us," Owen jested.

"It would have been nicer had we not, but what can you do?" I shrugged, still trying to swallow back my frustration. Being angry at Hailey wasn't going to help my cause.

Allie groaned, making us all laugh.

"Relax, no one cares that you are finally done playing hard to get." Jared seemed to like pushing her buttons as much as I did. She seemed like the type of girl who liked to stand up for herself, so I let it ride, but I'd be ready to step in if it got out of line. "Oh, I wasn't playing at anything." She glared at him. "What's your problem?"

"My problem?" he asked with mock innocence. Jared was quite the character when he wanted to be.

"Yeah. Why can't you go five minutes without saying something obnoxious to me?"

Owen snorted.

Allie glanced at me, probably waiting to see what I would do. I did nothing. She had this, and I was enjoying the show. I'd never seen a girl stand up to Jared that way.

"Like you're any better. You can't even look me in the eye tonight."

"Yes, I can." She walked over to him, stopping only inches away, and stared him down. "See. I can look you in the eye."

"Levi, can you tell your girl to heel?" Jared said dryly before turning away and disappearing down the beach.

"Arggh! What the hell is his problem?" She yelled.

"Isn't it obvious?" Owen answered.

She turned to look at him. "What's obvious?"

"You took his wing man away."

"Oh, please!" Hailey laughed. "Jared is just being his annoying self."

Allie looked at me, and I only shrugged. "I'll talk to him if you want, but you seem perfectly capable of handling it yourself."

"Yes, I am. And anyway, I should really be getting back."

"Already?" I wasn't ready to say goodnight. Maybe this was just code to get me alone again? A guy could hope.

"Yeah, it's getting late. I have something called work tomorrow. Ever heard of it?" She snapped.

"What, you think I don't have a job?" Did she think I was lazy or something?

"Do you?"

I went with evasive honesty. "I work for my father too."

"Oh."

"See, we have even more in common than you thought." I smiled. Allie looked so damn sexy when she was angry. That only reminded me of what had just been interrupted. "All right, I'll take you home."

"Good seeing you." Hailey tossed Allie's flip-flops over to her. She held them in one hand and took my advice this time. She looked adorable in my oversized sweatshirt. "You look too good in that." I moved behind her and pulled her into my arms.

"Bye!" she called to Hailey and Owen just as I took off.

I enjoyed the flight just as much this time. Having my hands on her was always nice, but the best part was that I knew she loved flying—she loved doing something that other guys couldn't give her.

We landed on her balcony, and I jimmied her door open. "This was an interesting night."

"Did you just break into my room?" she asked from behind me.

I pushed open the door. "Yeah, but the lock will still work, I promise."

"Except for one key problem."

"Which is?" I asked.

"It won't keep you out."

"Like you want that, babe," I teased.

She groaned. "Do you realize how frustrating you are?"

"Of course I do, but I like you all flustered and hot."

"Okay, shut up and get out of here."

"No goodnight kiss? Maybe a night cap?" I couldn't get enough of pushing her. Her reactions were priceless.

She seemed to fight some inner turmoil. I took that as a good sign.

"Goodnight, Levi."

I shrugged. "Oh well, see you in your dreams."

As I took off I heard her murmur, "So much for swearing off men."

My heart soared. I was in.

Chapter Four

It was her. I knew it in every grain of my body. I also knew that if I told her how I knew, she'd run away screaming. Allie was into me. Everything about her reactions supported that, but being into me and being interested in being my mate, were two different things.

I needed to keep things light, keep things about having a fun summer relationship until she was so hooked on me she wouldn't care what I asked of her.

I had a meeting with my dad at the hotel in the morning, and I found I didn't mind as much as usual. At least it meant I might get a second to see Allie.

I made it to the hotel a full twenty minutes early, but before I could so much as step inside I was waylaid by my dad's senior advisors. They seemed to always have something urgent to discuss with me.

As we walked through the front door I caught a quick glimpse of Allie. I couldn't stop to talk to her without opening her up to some serious questioning, so I hurried to the elevator.

The meetings dragged on all morning. We discussed nothing of major significance, just some foreign affairs that I could care less about. All I wanted to do was see Allie, but I feigned the minimal amount of interest to keep my father happy. I'd care more when it was actually time for me to take the reins. Until I was king, I was perfectly content staying out of things.

I waited until late afternoon to visit her again. I needed to play things cool. She seemed to enjoy the game of chase, but it was the kind of game that was all about the timing.

She noticed me seconds after I'd walked through the front doors of the hotel. Her eyes set on me, and I returned her gaze with a smile and wave as I made my way over to the desk.

"Hello there, beautiful. How was your day?" I leaned one elbow on the desk directly in front of her.

She didn't look at me. Instead she seemed to be watching something behind me. "It was work. I had a nice lunch though."

"Did you have company for this nice lunch or was it solo?"

"I had company." She continued looking behind me, and I needed to see for myself.

I turned to see the dark haired bartender. I drew in a breath. Did she really have lunch with this guy? Maybe I shouldn't have given her so much space. I wouldn't be making that mistake again. "Do you want to hang out tonight?"

"No, thanks." She turned her back on me and started toward the back office.

I moved behind the desk and gently touched her shoulder before she could go too far. "Am I missing something? What's up?"

She pursed her lips. "You're not actually allowed back here you know."

"Why don't you want to hang out? I thought you had fun yesterday." Was it because of that guy? I could feel my jealousy rise just like bile in my throat.

"Yeah, it was fun. But that doesn't mean I want to hang out every night."

"Okay, what happened? Is it him?" I pointed at the bartender.

"No!"

I relaxed. "Then what is it?"

"Why does there have to be a reason? Is it that impossible to believe that I'm not interested?"

Was she really going to play that card again? "You are interested. Don't bother to deny it. You weren't faking it on the beach."

"Could you lower your voice?" She hissed.

Then something dawned on me. She'd been happy to see me earlier. "Wait, this isn't about this morning is it?"

"Well…"

I relaxed further. It was just a misunderstanding. "Oh, I can explain that. I told you I work for my dad, those men I was with are his advisors. I figured you didn't need to meet them."

"Oh…"

"But wow, I'm flattered that it got to you," I teased. I was relieved she was only upset about my so-called brush off.

"Don't push it." Her voice had an edge to it. I had a feeling it had more to do with embarrassment than genuine annoyance.

I decided to move the conversation to a more enjoyable place. "So… tonight?"

She crossed her arms. "No thanks."

"Wait, I thought we cleared everything up?"

"It doesn't really matter. I still don't feel like going out."

"Then we can stay in… I can bring over some DVDs, or we could order something."

"You want to stay in and watch a movie?" she asked incredulously.

"Sure, why not? Besides, it's a good excuse to get into your room." I grinned.

"As tempting as it sounds, I'm going to pass."

I sighed. She was making this so much harder than it needed to be. "Okay, then what are you doing tomorrow morning?"

"I'm working…"

"Could you get out of it?"

"Depends on what for." She was definitely curious. That was a start.

"It's another surprise, but this time wear jeans and tennis shoes."

"Where would we go that I would need those?"

"You'll see." I kissed her on the cheek and left before she could change her mind about the next day. I'd miss her that night, but I also knew I couldn't push things too hard—yet.

***

"We're going out tonight." Jared didn't always grasp the fact that he answered to me and not the other way around. Eventually he'd have to accept it, but for the time being I didn't mind too much. He'd been my friend since before I had many memories. I had no plans to take over my dad's job without him staying around.

"Are we?" I took a seat on the couch across from him. I was already mentally going over the lists of long movies that could help me keep my mind off Allie for at least a few hours.

"Yes. You've been a hermit since meeting that girl. I get it, she's hot, but if she's not giving you any why not find it elsewhere?"

Anger boiled in me. As if I could find some temporary replacement for Allie? "I don't want anyone else. I'm taking my time with her. She's worth it."

"She's also just here for a few months."

"Maybe, maybe not. Either way, I'm not interested in screwing around with someone else."

"You can still go out."

"So I can watch you pick up girls? That does sound entertaining, but I think I'll pass."

"What are you going to do instead? Stalk the poor girl?"

"No, I'll probably just take a flight and get out of town for awhile."

"Bullshit. You won't leave town because you won't leave her."

He had me there. "All right, I'm game for a few drinks." I'd be seeing her the next day anyway.

"Nice. Ready now?"

"I need to stop by the hotel again—not to see her. I forgot something in my Dad's office."

"By forgot you mean you purposely left it there so you'd have an acceptable excuse to check on the girl again."

"Her name is Allie."

"Funny, I haven't heard you call her that."

I didn't bother to answer. Instead I walked outside and took flight.

Chapter Five

The basement was as dark as it always was as I wound my way over toward my Dad's office. I froze. I heard voices in the distance.

"It's not my place. You should talk to Levi if you want answers." Natalie? The manager wasn't often down in the basement even if she was a Pteron. "Because he's the one who brought you in."

"Brought me in? You mean like in on the secret?" Allie's voice made me freeze. What was she doing down here?

I quickly followed the voices over to the chamber and watched them from the doorway.

"Yes, he must really think you're special." Natalie smiled.

"I guess, but I don't know what makes me different from the rest of the girls he dates."

"The key word is dates. He has never really dated anyone seriously as far as I know. He's usually more of a one date kind of man."

"You mean he's a player?" There was a definite edge to her words.

"That's one way of putting it."

Allie raised an eyebrow. "I know that. I'm not letting myself get too attached." That was something I'd have to change. For the first time I regretted my history with women. I didn't want Allie questioning whether I was interested in anyone else.

"I'm not telling you that to scare you off. I'm letting you know he's been different with you, that's all."

Allie suddenly looked worried, "Are you going to tell Levi I was down here?"

Natalie looked right at me. She'd known I was listening in. "I won't have to."

"What do you mean?"

It was time to let Allie know I was there. I left the shadows of the doorway and joined the women. "Doing some exploring?"

Allie watched me carefully. "All right, you got me."

"Natalie, can we have a minute?" I gave the Pteron a look. I knew she wouldn't question me.

"Sure. I'll see you at work tomorrow morning?" Natalie asked Allie, but her eyes shifted to me.

"Allie won't be at work tomorrow. We have plans."

Allie's mouth dropped open. I bit back a smile. I loved surprising her.

"Of course. Goodnight." Natalie quickly hurried out of the room.

Allie stared after her. I had a feeling she was debating whether to follow. She didn't.

I closed the gap between us. Allie shivered, and I knew some of it was from fear. I never wanted to scare her, but she needed to be careful exploring The Society chambers like that.

"What am I going to do with you? You ever heard the saying 'curiosity killed the cat'?"

She said nothing. She kept her eyes fixed on me.

"I think I know what to do."

She tensed.

"Are you afraid?"

"Maybe," she whispered as she shivered again.

I leaned toward her. She closed her eyes before my lips made contact with hers. She opened her eyes and pulled away.

I laughed. "You were actually scared, weren't you?"

"Give me a break, Levi, it's creepy down here and I really know almost nothing about you. Of course you scared me."

"Well, you're not going to learn anything down here. Let's go upstairs." The only thing she'd find down here was trouble. I tried to play it off, but if my dad had been the one to find her, it wouldn't have gone over so well.

"At least tell me what this room is for."

"It's for meetings, Al. You happy?"

"Meetings? Is that really all you are going to give me?"

"Listen, I'd tell you more but then I'd have to kill you, and I already scared you enough for tonight."

"Levi!"

"Okay, okay. What do you want to know?"

"Everything. What is this? How do the Pterons fit in? Were you joking when you said there were actually vampires? What else is there—?"

"Whoa. Slow down there, babe. I can't answer them all at once." Her curiosity was a good thing. If she was going to be my mate she'd have to become part of The Society. My mate. Those two words took on new meaning now that I had a face to put with the intense dream that had been haunting me for years.

"Well, you have to start somewhere."

"Does it have to be here? I can think of a few more comfortable places to discuss this."

"If this is another attempt to get into my room, forget it."

I decided to give her something. "Fine. This is the meeting room for The Society. The Pterons oversee it, but the council includes members from several different shifter groups. Lower lying groups like the vampires don't have seats."

"Vampires are low lying?" Her eyes widened in surprise.

"They suck blood from people, how much more of a bottom dweller can you imagine?"

"True. But I don't know… they seem more glamorous in books and movies."

"Yes, because books and movies always get things right." I shook my head. Popular culture always got paranormal creatures wrong. They usually left us out because they didn't know about us. I liked it that way.

"Fine. So why are the Pterons in charge?"

"We're the most powerful. Our hybrid form helps, as does our strength." If she only knew what role I was going to play in The Society.

"So is your strength one of those abilities you promised to tell me about later?"

"Yes. Not that it should surprise you." I folded my arms across my chest. Her eyes zeroed in on my biceps.

"No, I guess it isn't surprising." She smiled, and I knew she was thinking about what I looked like without a shirt on.

"If that about answers your questions, what do you say we get out of here?"

"This isn't over, but I'll take what I can get for tonight."

I walked her to the elevator, making sure she really left. I grabbed the papers I needed from Dad's office—the ones that probably could have sat there for another two days. I enjoyed sharing more of The Society with Allie, especially since she seemed to like it more than I did.

***

"It's so cool that you've spent time in France."

I tried to tune out the girl hanging all over me, but she was particularly difficult to shrug off.

"Sure. It's cool."

"I've always wanted to go there. I mean I've been to Europe, but only the England part."

I resisted the urge to roll my eyes. The England part? I didn't want to mess with Jared's attempt to get this girl's friend in bed, but I also wasn't going to go out of my way to help. "Yeah."

"And you're a senior in college?"

I didn't even bother to answer that one. The girl was grasping at straws.

"Levi?" The girl put a hand on my shoulder, and I shrugged it off. Having any other girl's hands on me felt wrong. "Are you okay? You seem distracted."

"I am distracted."

"Is there anything I can do to help?" She put a hand on my leg.

I shrugged off her hand, again. "Not at all."

"Oh." She sounded disappointed.

"Listen, you seem like a nice enough girl. I'm going to lay it out there for you. I'm not interested."

Jared glared.

I shot him a look of his own. "What? Don't act surprised."

"Who is she?" Finally the blonde made a statement I cared about answering.

"She's perfect."

"She's lucky." The girl stood up. "And I'm done wasting my time."

"Jamie!" Her friend slipped out of Jared's arm and followed her out.

"Thanks for that, man. Real helpful." Jared downed his beer.

"I told you I wasn't interested in messing around with anyone else."

"That doesn't mean you can't play along for my sake."

"Yes it does." I pushed away my half full beer. I didn't want it.

"It's her isn't it? The girl from your dream."

I let out a deep breath. "It's her."

"Are you sure? Absolutely positive?"

"Yes. I felt it last night. She's the one."

"I knew it." He leaned back in his chair. "I knew it."

"You knew she was my mate? For how long?"

"From the beginning—from the way you've obsessed over her every movement." He no longer seemed angry, more resolved.

"And you're just telling me this now?"

"I thought I'd let you figure this out yourself." He stood up.

"I'm sure. Leaving already?"

"You want to run by the hotel and check on her, don't you?"

"What does it mean that I want to?"

"That you're a lost cause."

"A lost cause? Is that a bad thing?

"A horrible thing for me—but not so bad for you." He stalked out of the bar.

Chapter Six

I waited for her by the front entrance of the hotel. I'd barely slept the night before—luckily I only needed a few hours of sleep at most per night. I hoped she appreciated my less than typical plans for the day.

"Good morning, beautiful." I smiled when she approached me. I'd missed her. I was losing it completely.

"Good morning. Sleep well?"

Was she teasing me? Did she realize the torture I went through the night before holding myself back from visiting her. "I slept well, and you?"

"I slept wonderfully."

"Any dreams?" I had to ask.

"Yes. I actually had some nice ones."

"About anyone I know?"

"Maybe." She smiled coyly.

"Whoever was in them was a lucky guy."

"Yeah, well. I'll have to tell him you said that."

I let my arm brush against hers. "You do that."

I led her outside, and she headed straight for my car. She waited by the passenger door of my black BMW.

"How'd you know it was mine?"

"You said you were parked down here, and it seemed more you than an old Civic or a pickup." She watched me. She wanted to know what I thought about her analysis of me.

"I like how you don't hold back, Al. You just say it like it is."

"So you are really sticking to the Al thing, huh?"

"It fits."

"Whatever." She tried to shrug it off, but I saw the smile she attempted to hide.

I opened the passenger door for her, and I made sure she was buckled before walking around to the driver side.

"Are you ready to tell me where we're going?

I started the car. "Patience, patience."

She yawned. It was a cute yawn that made me wonder exactly what kind of dreams she was having the night before.

I drove while forcing my eyes to stay on the road. I enjoyed having her in the passenger seat next to me. It felt so completely natural. I came to a stop along the curb of what probably looked like a typical construction site.

"Seriously? Do I seem like the type to like construction work?"

"No, but I think you'll like this." I smiled. She said she wanted to know more about me, and she was about to get what she asked for.

"Okay…" She stepped out of the car carefully. She still had no clue what I had planned for her.

A man in a hardhat greeted us as we walked closer to the house. "Levi, you made it."

I nodded at the familiar face. "Hi, Phil. Of course. I brought another set of hands with me."

"I can see that."

"Allie, this is Phil. Phil, Allie."

"Nice to meet you." Allie accepted his outstretched hand.

"The pleasure is all mine. We are always looking for new volunteers."

"Volunteers?" She glanced around, understanding finally setting in.

"Yes. We've been doing rebuilding work since the storm, but it seems there is always more work to be done."

"I'm sure." By her reaction I guessed she knew he meant Katrina. This was a rebuilding project.

"Do you know how to use a hammer?" I was more curious about her answer than you'd expect.

"I can't say I've ever used one, but I'm game to try."

***

"Having fun?" I eyed Allie looking sexier than ever wearing a tool-belt around her slender waist. I offered her a bottle of water.

She accepted the water and opened the top. "Yeah, I actually am. It seems I have a hidden talent for hammering nails, huh?"

"It seems so." I took a swig of water from my own bottle. We'd been working for hours in the sticky summer heat. "We can head out if you want. I think Hailey wanted to steal you later."

"Steal me?" She tied her hair up in a bun on the top of her head. The action exposed her neck. The temptation to kiss her there was hard to resist. Everything with Allie was hard to resist.

"Absolutely, today was all mine, remember?"

"Do you do this a lot?" She asked.

"Usually once or twice a month. I did more right after Katrina, but I never really stopped."

"I'm glad you brought me."

"See, I'm not all bad." She needed to believe me. She needed to get to know the real me—at least the part I could show her.

"No, only 90%," she teased.

"Ouch, this only buys me 10%?" I undid her tool belt and slipped it off.

"What can I say, I have expensive taste."

"I'll keep that in mind."

Chapter Seven

"What happened?" I barked into the phone before Hailey could get more than a few words out. All I'd been told was that there had been an incident involving Allie, Hailey, and some sort of carjacker with a gun. I was hoping it was all some mistake, but by the speed at which Hailey picked up the phone, I knew it wasn't.

"A guy tried to steal my car, and I took care of it." Hailey sounded so calm on the surface, but I could feel the anxiety under her voice. She was shaken up by the experience, and not for fear of her own wellbeing. She was worried about Allie. She was also afraid—of me.

"First of all. It's not your fault. Let's just get that out of the way so we can talk about the real issue. Is she okay? Was she scared?" This was why I shouldn't have let her out of my sight. What if she hadn't been with Hailey? What if the creep had tried to hurt her when she was unprotected?

"She's okay, but yes she was freaked out. I'm not sure if she was more upset about the guy holding a gun on us or what I did to him though."

"Clearly she knows about our strength now." I tried to act calm, but I was anything but. The thought of some scum bag pointing a gun at my Allie made my blood just about boil over.

"That she does."

"I need to see her." At least it was dark out. I could be at her hotel in minutes if I flew.

"For once I agree with you." Hailey sighed. "She could use some comforting and you're the one to do it."

"Glad we see eye to eye on this one." I hung up the phone and made the short flight to the hotel. I landed on Allie's balcony. I couldn't be bothered with going around through the front. Even Hailey thought Allie needed me, and I wasn't going to wait a second longer than I had to.

I retracted my wings and knocked lightly on the glass door. I assumed she'd figure out it was me and not freak out.

She pulled back the curtains and my eyes locked with hers. For the millionth time her green eyes nearly took my breath away. This time her eyes were scared—I hated that look on her face.

She held open the door for me, and I immediately walked in closing the door behind me.

"What are you doing here?" she snapped. I knew it was out of fear and nerves rather than actual anger at my appearance.

She looked sexy yet vulnerable standing there in what I assumed was pajamas. The shorts were wonderfully short and the cami left little to the imagination. No matter how great my imagination was, I wanted to tear away the remaining fabric. But that's not why I was there. "I heard what happened and wanted to make sure you were okay."

"I'm fine." She pressed her lips firmly together. "But it was thoughtful of you to come."

"Well, I'm glad you decided to let me in tonight, last time you practically slammed the door in my face." I grinned, hoping to lighten the mood for both of us.

"I guess tonight's your lucky night." She seemed to notice her slip of the tongue. "Um, scratch that. Not lucky in that way. Fine, I'm glad you're here. Tonight was pretty scary. I mean Hailey took care of the situation quickly but I've never had someone pull a gun on me before." She started to shake and all I wanted to do was hold her and make it stop.

Instead I settled for using words. "It's okay. I promise that guy has been taken care of." I'd be paying the scum bag a visit myself.

"What do you mean?" She spoke slowly like she was afraid of the answer. She probably should have been.

"He's been apprehended. Leave it at that."

"Okay…"

"Come here." I sat down on the couch and opened my arms for her. I was done holding back. Evidently so was she. Without a moment of hesitation she fell into my arms, leaning her head on my chest.

I gently kissed the top of her head. "It's normal to be scared. Not everyone is like Hailey and can just let something like that slide. Don't fight it."

I just sat there holding her, listening and feeling her every breath. I was soothing her, and I wasn't sure if I'd ever experienced such a satisfying feeling. "Do you want me to stay?"

She hesitated with her answer, and for one small moment I thought she'd say yes.

"No, I'll be fine."

"If it makes you feel any better, this hotel is probably the safest place in the city." The basement was watched 24/7, which meant the whole hotel was. Any unsuspecting criminal who tried to break into the Crescent City Hotel would be in for a rude awakening.

As easily as I could have persuaded her, I let it go. I didn't want to be pushy. I wanted to be comforting.

"Oh." She picked her head up off my chest and smiled reassuringly. "It does make me feel better."

"Call me if you need anything or you just want to talk." I stood up and walked toward the balcony door before pausing. "Thanks, by the way."

"For?"

"The image. I was wondering what you slept in. Goodnight, Al."

As I disappeared into the night I heard the echo of her voice. "Goodnight, Levi." That whisper stayed with me the whole flight home.

Chapter Eight

I only stayed home about ten minutes before I left again. I wanted to give our interrogators enough time with the human who had made the mistake of breaking into the wrong car, but it didn't take long for me to get tired of waiting. Jared was already down at the interrogation rooms with his father. I had to suffer through meetings, and he had to be present for all major security events. His job seemed a lot of a lot more fun than mine. I walked out of my room and found Owen pacing in the hall.

"Are you ready to go?" Owen didn't need me to tell him where I was going.

"Yes. You should have seen her, man. She's seriously freaked out."

"Hailey feels awful."

"It's not her fault."

"No, it was his." Owen clenched his hand into his fist. He was angry that someone would mess with Hailey. She might have had superhuman strength, but she was still his baby sister.

We made the short flight over to The Society's less appealing offices that were across the river in Algiers. Being brought into one of these rooms wasn't a good thing for anyone.

I heard my father's commanding voice before I saw him. I steadied myself. I was in for questions. Considering the anger I already felt, dealing with my father wasn't high on my list.

"Dad." I acknowledged him as soon as we reached the hallway outside the interrogation room.

"Levi." He nodded at me. "I assume you've heard about the incident?"

"Of course I did."

"Who is she to you?" His eyes locked on mine. "Evidently she's important."

"Don't you know? I assume you're only here for that reason."

"I'm here because this is my building. I am still king, Levi."

"And I hope you stay king a long while."

He sighed. "I'm not going down this road with you again. We have more important things to worry about."

"Like what?" I eyed the door, ready to give the guy a piece of my mind.

He looked at Owen. "This conversation doesn't get repeated."

"That goes without saying, sir." Owen was good at kissing my dad's ass.

"The human wasn't acting alone."

"What?" Dad suddenly had my interest.

"Jet broke him. He was hired indirectly by the Blackwells."

"Blackwells?" I couldn't have heard him right, although I wasn't surprised that Jett, Jared's Dad was able to make him talk. He wasn't the head of security for nothing.

"Why would the Blackwells have sent anyone after Hailey, especially a weak human?" The Blackwells were a rival Pteron family that had been gunning for the crown for years.

Dad glared. "Are you going to play dumb?"

"Allie? You think they were after Allie?"

"His job was to report back information. Evidently Hailey caught him just after he placed a tracking device."

"But why Allie? She's just a human."

"She stopped being just a human when you took an interest in her." Dad stared hard at me before turning to Owen. "Do me a favor, find Jett and tell him I need to speak to him as soon as possible."

Owen nodded at both of us and walked away.

Dad waited until he was out of ear shot to continue. "Let's cut to the chase. The Blackwells know it's time for you to find a mate. Suddenly you start spending all your time with her. What conclusion do you think they're going to come to?"

"Just because I spend time with a girl, doesn't mean I'm taking her as my mate." I wasn't going to admit he was right. Not yet. There was still so much to figure out.

"You can say anything you want, but for once in your life you will not screw up. I'm putting extra security on her, but I assure you they won't interrupt your courting."

"Courting?" I rolled my eyes.

"Would you prefer I used a more vulgar term?"

"No. But I need to talk to the guy. If he was after Allie I need to get at him."

"No." Dad crossed his arms. "You're not making this worse. Leave it to the security team."

"How am I supposed to become King when you won't let me get involved?"

"The Kings job isn't to get his hands dirty."

"Don't go near her."

He put a hand on my shoulder. "I won't go near her if you do what you're supposed to. I know you don't approve of everything I do, and you like to fight me every turn, but this isn't about you and me. This is about The Society, and it's about the girl. I don't need to tell you what could happen to her if she got into the Blackwells' hands."

I felt my body ready to transform. No one was touching Allie.

"I changed my mind. Go ahead and see the guy. Maybe we can send him back to the Blackwells with a message." Dad turned on his heels just as the door to the interrogation room opened and Jared walked out. "He's all ready for you, man."

"Thanks." I walked in, completely clear on just what message I'd be sending.

***

I was beginning to think Allie was a magnet for trouble. Either that or Hailey was looking for ways to get on my bad side. Maybe it was a combination of both.

"You found what?" Owen barked into his phone as he sat in the passenger seat of my car.

I heard his mother clearly on the other end of the phone. "Hailey went to a Were party. I found the invite on her computer. She said she was hanging out with a girlfriend, so she didn't go alone."

I gripped the steering wheel tighter. Hailey and Allie had plans. "Allie. She took my Allie to a Were party?" I struggled to contain my anger. She wouldn't be at the party for long. The Blackwells' new interest made me even more concerned for her safety.

"Is that Levi?" Owen's mother asked.

"Yeah. Allie's kind of his girlfriend."

Girlfriend. That was a new one for me, but the term didn't say enough for how I already felt about her.

"Oh. Well then she's even crazier than I thought. You'll go get her?"

"Yes. You sure it's at that warehouse?"

I didn't wait to hear more before making an abrupt turn. "Call Jared and tell him to meet us there." We wouldn't need him, but it didn't hurt to show up prepared.

Jared met us right outside the large industrial building. "Does your sister have a death wish, Owen?"

"I'm beginning to think so." Owen shook his head. "I don't know what's gotten into her."

"I'm all about them being friends, but putting Allie in danger isn't acceptable." I instantly regretted not telling Hailey the truth about the carjacker.

"What's the plan? Are we just flying in?" Jared was already checking out the perimeter. He'd make a great head of security when the time came.

"Yes. I don't want her at this party a second more than necessary." I didn't want Allie to think I didn't trust her, but keeping her safe was more important than worrying about that. She was human, and even with Hailey around she was far too vulnerable.

I gave both of my friends a nod, and we flew up to the roof. It only took a moment to assess the situation. A wolf was grabbing her. A Were had his dirty hands on her. He dared to touch my future mate.

"Put your damn paws on her again, and you'll be short one." I reached around her from behind and wrapped my arms around her waist protectively.

The Were sneered at me. "Oh, hi Levi. I didn't realize you hadn't had this one yet. What do you care anyway, don't you usually go for the humans?"

I pushed Allie behind me, tucking her in between Jared and Owen. I stepped toward the idiot. "Humans are superior to you lowlifes." But he had said usually go for humans. Did he think Allie was something else?

"You have the nerve to come to my party and insult me?"

"I can insult you anywhere I want, *dog*." Calling a wolf shifter a dog was a sure fire way to piss them off. Even so, his anger would be nothing compared to mine. I felt my body ready to transform. I knew my eyes were turning black and my wings were prepared to break free. I was positive the others were doing the same.

Seconds later a large wolf stood in front of me. Unlike Pterons, wolf shifters change completely. Pterons are the only ones that maintain our human form.

My wings broke free. "Stay with Allie and don't move," I yelled at Hailey. She nodded.

A line of grey wolves joined the first, and the leader snarled at me.

My response was swift. I picked him up by the scruff of his neck and tossed him. "Anyone else going to dare to disrespect me?" I screamed, my hands balling into fists. "You do not touch our women. Do you understand?"

No one said anything.

"Let's go!" I pulled Allie to my side and wrapped my arms around her waist before jumping off the building. I wanted her as far away from those wolves as possible.

I released her as soon as we reached the ground, and I spun on Hailey. "What the hell were you thinking? A Were party? What, you slumming it now? And you thought it was acceptable to take Allie with you? Are you dense?" I just kept picturing that wolf pawing at her.

Hailey met my gaze head on. "We were having fun until you showed up."

"And what would you have done if that punk tried to push things further with Allie?" I seethed. I tried to go easy on Hailey when I could, but this was crossing the line.

"I would have protected her. I can take care of myself and her."

"What, now that you have your full strength you think you're invincible?" I didn't bother to control my anger. She needed to learn.

"Get real, Hailey. You might be stronger than a Were, but there is nothing you could have done against a whole party of those guys." Jared backed me up. What Hailey had done was inexcusable. If she hadn't been Owen's sister and a friend of Allie's she would have been facing some serious trouble.

Allie held up her hands. "Stop it! Stop yelling at her. I decided to come with her, so it's my fault too."

I wrung my hands and turned to Allie. "It's not your fault, but I do wish you had bothered to tell me where you were going."

"Since when do I have to check in with you every time I go out?"

"Since you decided to spend time with Weres. You have no idea how dangerous they can be." My anger was being replaced by worry. What if we'd been too late and the wolf had tried something more?

"Not as dangerous as you."

"The difference is I'm not going to hurt you. They would."

"Can we just go home?" she pleaded. Hailey now looked completely defeated and there was no reason to keep haranguing her. Luckily Allie was fine.

"Of course, I'll take you home."

"Flying?"

"I have my car." For once I was glad to have the car as an excuse. I needed time alone with her and driving would take longer.

Allie turned around. "Is that okay, Hailey?"

"It's fine." Hailey wisely waved her on.

I wrapped my arm around Allie's waist and led her toward my car.

As we walked away I heard Owen talking to Hailey. "You can't talk to him like that! You have to respect him. Mom and Dad would kill you if they heard you talking that way."

I hoped Allie wouldn't read too much into that statement.

I pulled her into a hug, I needed her close. "Are you all right? I didn't think to ask before."

"I'm fine. I have a lot of questions, but I'm fine."

"Can the questions wait?" I asked. My body was still calming down from the confrontation.

"For tonight, but you can't put them off forever."

"Are you sure about that?"

"Completely."

I opened her door for her before going around to my side.

Just as I pulled away from the curb she turned to me. "Okay, can I at least ask one question?"

I nodded. "I don't have a choice, do I?"

"How'd you know where we were?"

"Why, are you worried I'm following you now?"

"Not exactly, I just need to know." Not exactly? Would it have bothered her?

"It's nothing that dramatic. Hailey left the email about the party open on her computer. Her mom found it and called Owen to get her."

"Oh…"

"So, no more questions for tonight then?"

"Could I ask one more?"

I glanced over at her as we sat at a red light. I held her hand in her lap. "You're a hard girl to say no to."

"Who are you, Levi? What is it that you're not telling me?"

I held on to her hand but turned my eyes back to the road. "No more questions. It's late and I need to get you home."

I knew the questions were just going to continue, but I wasn't ready to give her all the answers yet. How long could I hold her off? The summer was flying by.

Chapter Nine

I knocked on Allie's door, already missing her after a day. I was losing it, and there was absolutely nothing I could do.

The door opened, but it wasn't Allie standing there.

The attractive woman bore a striking resemblance to Allie, but she was probably around twenty years older. "Well, hello there."

"Oh, hi. Is Allie around?" I checked the room number again even though I'd already deduced the woman had to be her mom.

Allie materialized in the doorway. "Hey."

"Hey." I looked at her while waiting for my introduction.

"Aren't you going to introduce us, sweetie?" Evidently her mother had the same idea.

"Oh yeah, Mom this is Levi."

"It's so nice to meet you Ms.—" I held out my hand at a loss for her mother's last name. I knew her parents were divorced, and I wasn't sure whether she'd gone back to a maiden name. That wasn't something I wanted to mess up on our first meeting.

"It's O'Connor but call me Diane."

"Well it's nice to meet you, Diane. I've heard a lot about you."

"Have you? Funny, I haven't heard anything about you. Unless, is this the friend I didn't need to concern myself with?" Diane gave Allie an unmistakable look. She hadn't even mentioned me to her mother? I tried not to let the disappointment get to me. Maybe she wasn't the kind of girl who told her mother about her love life—but to say I was a friend? That stung.

Allie just stared at both of us with a deer in headlights look on her face.

I couldn't just stand there. "Well, I'll let you enjoy your time with your mother. Call me sometime. Once again, nice to meet you."

"Wait, Levi. Do you have plans tomorrow night?" Diane turned to me. "We would love to have you join us for dinner. Allie's father will be there as well."

I reacted on instinct. I could make the dinner work for me. "I would love to join you for dinner. What time were you thinking?"

"Around seven o'clock down in the lobby?"

"Perfect, I look forward to it. Good night, Allie." I made no effort to put her at ease. Calling me a friend wasn't cool—not at all.

***

I waited for Allie and her parents in the lobby of the hotel the next night. I'd given her space, assuming she'd appreciate the time with her mom. For the first time in my life I was nervous about meeting someone. Meeting her mother was hard enough, but her dad? I still hadn't talked to Allie about her failure to tell her mother about me. I figured I'd just have to take things into my own hands to move them in the right direction.

I was reading an angry email from my dad when I sensed Allie and her family approaching. I quickly pocketed my phone and took another inventory of how I looked. A collared shirt and khaki slacks seemed appropriate for the occasion.

I walked the few steps to meet them. "Hi Allie, Diane. Mr. Davis, it's nice to finally meet you. I'm Levi."

Her father held out his hand. "Hello, Levi, please call me Tim."

"All right, Tim." I accepted the firm handshake.

"So you're the one my little girl has been spending all her time with?"

Nice. At least her dad knew about me.

I relaxed and smiled at him. "Yes, I have been monopolizing her attention all summer. I just can't seem to get enough of her."

"Allie told you about Levi?" Diane put a hand on her hip. The mannerism made her look so similar to her daughter.

"She didn't have to tell me. I know what's going on in my daughter's life. I'm sorry she didn't feel the need to share it with you." Tim seemed pleased with himself. I didn't know much about the current state of things with Allie's parents, but there was some serious tension.

Diane pursed her lips. "She didn't actually tell you then?"

"Not exactly," Tim said through clenched teeth.

"So how did you hear?"

"Oy vey, Diane. You got me. No one actually told me, I only assumed."

"Just like I thought." Diane smiled smugly.

So much for Allie telling her Dad.

Allie gave me a fleeting 'I'm sorry' look. "Okay, let's get to dinner before someone gets killed."

"Good idea." I put an arm around Allie as we headed toward the entrance. I leaned in to whisper in her ear. "Is this okay, *friend*?"

"Please don't start," she pleaded quietly.

As much as I wanted to reassure her, I needed her to know I wasn't playing games. I wasn't just her friend, and we both knew it. I also wasn't disappearing from her life. She'd have to let me get to know her parents eventually. "Oh, I haven't gotten started yet, babe."

"Lovely."

We were given a corner table at the Palace Café. It wasn't a bad spot, but it wasn't the best seat in the house. If it had been just Allie and me, I would have complained, but I decided not to rock the boat with her parents. I pulled out Allie's chair for her just as her father pulled out

Diane's. I was rewarded with a nod. Would he expect anything less of a man dating his daughter?

Allie and her mother were having some silent conversation I couldn't quite read. I knew Allie was close to her mother, but there was definitely some strain there. I had a feeling it was about me.

Tim ordered a bottle of wine. As soon as the waiter left he looked at me. "So Levi, are you in school or have you graduated?"

"I'm about to start my senior year at Tulane." Hopefully he wouldn't have an issue with the age difference.

"Any plans yet for after graduation?" he asked. He was sizing me up. As a business man himself he probably wanted to make sure his daughter was dating someone ambitious.

Allie touched his arm. "Dad, you don't need to interrogate him."

I smiled. I had no problem with the line of questioning. "It's fine. I don't mind in the slightest. I'm going to be working in the family business."

"And what kind of business is that?" Tim's eyes brightened. I had his interest.

"It's a large diversified corporation. We've got hands in a lot of places." I kept things very broad and vague.

"Sounds a lot like my own. What did you say the name was?"

"I didn't. It's the Laurent Corporation." I waited for his response. The name meant a lot in the business world.

His face reddened. "Oh wow, I had no idea."

I smiled. I'd just gone up a few notches in his book.

"Will your business keep you in New Orleans, Levi? Any plans to spend time in the Northeast after graduation?"

"We're very locally based, but there are some travel opportunities if I'm inclined." I was hoping to keep Allie in New Orleans, but I'd do what I had to.

"I see." Diane smiled lightly. I sensed she understood my feelings for Allie were nowhere near as casual as Allie had made them sound.

The waiter brought over the wine, and we ordered dinner. I wasn't particularly hungry. I was more concerned with how Allie was responding to everything. Her whole body was tense, and I wondered why the situation had her so wound up.

Diane broke an awkward silence that had set in. "How did you two meet?"

I smiled thinking about the first few times I saw her. "Your daughter first caught my eye in the lobby of the hotel, but I didn't have the pleasure of meeting her formally until I ran into her at a karaoke bar of all places."

"A karaoke bar?" Diane didn't hide her surprise well. I'd been right that singing publicly wasn't Allie's thing.

"Yes. Allie and her friend did a lovely rendition of *Girls Just Want to Have Fun*."

"I was wondering about that. Why isn't Jessica joining us tonight?" Tim gave Allie a sidelong glance.

Diane's face turned serious. "Do you mean to tell me you weren't aware that Jess left weeks ago? You had no idea of this when you left our daughter alone in a hotel suite on Bourbon Street of all places and with Casanova over there?" Diane pointed at me, and I smirked.

Allie exhaled loudly. "Mom, I'm starting college in the fall. I don't need to be babysat."

Diane set down her wine with a thump. "Princeton is not New Orleans."

"No it's not, but it's still unsupervised. Besides, I could have gone to college in New Orleans if I wanted."

I knew she was just using it to make a point, but would she consider it? Would changing her college plans appeal to her?

The anger on Diane's face had slowly melted into concern. "But you're not. Your father shouldn't have left you."

"What's done is done, it's not an issue. Now please can we enjoy the evening?" Allie sighed.

Before things could get more uncomfortable, our meals arrived. I tried to come up with a new conversation, but Tim took care of that himself.

"So where do you live, Levi? Are you on campus?"

That was an easy enough question to answer. "I only lived on campus one year. I live in an apartment with a few friends. It's a nice place. Isn't it, Allie?"

Allie kicked me under the table. I'd warned her I wasn't done making it clear just how much more than friends we were.

"Oh, Allie has seen it?" Diane took a slow sip of her wine.

I smiled at Allie. "Yes, she's spent plenty of evenings there."

Allie's expression was priceless. "Evenings meaning hanging out. The only time I stayed over was on the couch. Okay? Can we please change the subject?"

"Of course." I smiled. "So Diane, how long are you in town for?"

"I leave tomorrow morning. I only wanted to check in on Allie since no one else apparently is." She pushed some food around on her plate. Evidently I wasn't the only one without an appetite.

"Oh, that's too bad. I would have loved to introduce you to my parents."

"What?" Allie's mouth fell open. I loved taking her by surprise.

Diane set down her fork. "How thoughtful, that would have been nice."

"My parents know all about Allie and are so excited to meet her." I returned her stare. That wasn't exactly true. I did plan to tell my mother about her, but it's just that in my world it was a bit more complicated. And technically my father knew she existed.

"It's nice to hear you are close to your parents. I think communication between a parent and child is of extreme importance." Diane gave Allie a disapproving look. I felt a twinge of guilt. I didn't actually want to get her in trouble.

"Well, I'd like to meet your parents, Levi. Just name the time and place," Tim quickly replied.

I'm sure he would. Tim was seeing dollar signs. "I will. My parents will be thrilled."

"Excuse me." Allie threw down her napkin and pushed back her chair. She stormed off, and I hoped she was only going to the restroom.

Tim was the safer one to talk to, but Diane had more of the answers I needed.

I was about to start in with the questions when Tim turned to his wife. "I didn't know you were coming into town. You could have given me some warning."

"Warning? To visit my daughter? I had to make sure she was doing all right."

"And she's fine. I'm capable of taking care of her."

I tried to tune them out. It felt wrong to witness the fighting.

Thankfully a few moments later Allie returned with a grin, "Honey, we're going to be late, aren't we?"

"For what?" I watched her closer as she sat down. What was she playing at now?

"That thing we just couldn't miss." The look she shot me said it all. I needed to just go along with it.

"Oh yeah."

"Well, we don't want to keep you kids, let's get the check." Tim seemed to get it too. The guy had made his share of mistakes, but he understood when to just go with the flow.

Ten minutes later we headed for the door. Upstairs we hadn't noticed the start of a torrential rainstorm.

"I didn't know it was going to rain." Diane appeared reluctant to enter the downpour.

"It's just how things are here. It can go from a clear sky to a storm in minutes," Allie explained. I smiled. She was really getting used to New Orleans.

"We might as well get it over with." Tim didn't seem concerned. Either that or he just wanted to get away from the situation.

"Okay, thanks for dinner. I won't be back too late, Mom." Allie was also ready.

"All right, have a nice night you two." Diane waved before dashing out.

As soon as her parents disappeared, Allie tugged on my hand and walked right out into the rain. Instead of running back toward the hotel she stopped. "What the hell was all of that? What are you playing at?"

"What am I playing at? I can't believe you didn't tell your parents about me!" I finally let my feelings out. I wasn't much for blowing things out of proportion, but calling me her friend wasn't going to fly.

"What the heck was I supposed to tell them? It's not like we're officially together or anything."

I felt my blood boiling. Was she kidding me? We'd been together the whole damn summer. "Not officially together? You mean I've been staying away from other girls all summer just for the fun of it?"

Her body relaxed. Something in my words got through to her. "It's not like I've been with anyone else either."

I let my anger subside. It wasn't going to help anything. "Then what are we arguing about? That we're both too stubborn to admit we actually have something here?"

"What does it matter? I mean it's already August—"

No. She wasn't going there. I still had time. "Just stop. I know what the problem is."

"Care to enlighten me?"

It was time to step things up a notch. "Let me take you out on a real date."

"Seriously? That's your response? And what separates a real date from anything else?"

"Dinner, wine, nice clothes. Come on, it'll be fun."

She paused, and for a frightening second I thought she was going to say no. "Fine."

"So Friday night at seven?"

"Okay. Are we done here 'cause this rain is getting old and—"

Despite the rain, I could only concentrate on her face—on her lips. I interrupted her complaints by crushing my lips into hers. It wasn't gentle. I was done being gentle. She didn't seem to mind. She wrapped her arms around my neck and pulled my head down to her level. I explored her mouth, reveling in the sweet taste.

A honking car brought us back to reality, and I stepped back slowly. I wanted her. I needed her. But not like that. Not yet. "I guess I should get you out of the rain."

"You mean us?"

"No, just you. The rain doesn't bother me much." Besides, the cool water was helping my restraint.

"Why doesn't that surprise me?"

"With me babe, the surprises never end." I draped an arm over her shoulder and led her back to the hotel.

Chapter Ten

She couldn't leave. That much was clear. I needed her in my life, and she was destined to be my mate. I'd waited years for her. I'd spent years with just a hazy dream that felt more like a memory than something made up in my sub-conscious. I knew without anyone telling me that the vision was of the future, and if I wanted to get there—to a moment when my mate was with me truly and completely— I had to find a way to keep Allie at my side.

She wanted me. She opened up around me, she smiled more. I was as good for her as she was for me, but I needed to make sure she saw that. I needed to make sure she realized just how much I could and would offer her. But I couldn't tell her everything, at least not yet. Too much information too fast might scare her off.

I hadn't been over to my parents' house in a while. My father was away on business which left me blissfully free from his disapproving eye. I wasn't in the mood to deal with another lecture on my inadequacy. At least I'd found my mate. Everything else would fall into place.

My mom didn't hear me come in through the front door, so I went right upstairs. I was on a mission, and I didn't want to have to explain what I was doing to her. I was nervous enough about the monumental step I was about to take. I didn't need anyone trying to stop me. It was for that reason I hadn't told my friends. For once they both would have agreed on something, that I was an idiot. And maybe I'd have thought the same thing if it weren't for the way she made me feel—the way that memory ran through my mind on repeat, the way her body called to me constantly. And those eyes. Those damn green eyes that were my complete and utter undoing. And even my selfish reasons aside, I needed to keep her safe. As much as I hated to admit it, my father was right. She'd stopped being just a human the minute I took more than a passing interest in her. Turning back now was out of the question.

I walked into my old bedroom and went right over to the dresser. I opened the top drawer and searched for the ring. It wasn't there. A moment of panic hit me until I remembered. I'd taken the ring already, weeks before. I'd stuffed it in a pair of my slacks. Had I really forgotten? Allie was making me lose my mind.

I took the stairs back down two at a time.

"Levi?" Mom watched me from the entryway.

"Hi, Mom. Just getting something from my room."

"What did you get?" She looked me over, probably looking for evidence of what I'd taken.

"It wasn't here after all."

She crossed her arms and looked at me. "Do I need to know what you're up to?"

"No. Not at all." I couldn't waste time chatting. I needed to get home. I had to find that ring.

"Do you want to stay for dinner? I wasn't planning anything big since your father is away, but I can whip up something."

"Oh. No thanks. I have plans." I slipped passed her to the door. "Maybe another time."

I practically ran to my car, well aware that my mom was watching me. I didn't let it bother me. If things worked out the way I expected them to, she'd be very happy with me. I'd more than make up for blowing her off.

I raced back to my apartment in record time. I walked right by Jared, ignoring his questioning stare. I searched my closet. I checked the pockets of every pair of pants I owned. Nothing. I slammed my fist into the wall creating a large hole. I'd have to clean up the plaster later. Had I seriously fucked up that bad?

I thought about Allie. How close I was to getting exactly what I wanted. I had to find the ring. I glanced around and found exactly what I was looking for. Balled up on the floor by my desk were the pants, and the ruby ring was exactly where I'd left it.

I fished it out and carefully placed it in my night stand. Hopefully it would be securely on Allie's finger in just a few days. After that there was no way anyone was losing that ring.

***

I forced down my nerves as I knocked on her door. I'd spent so many nights doing the exact same thing, but that night was different. That night was going to end with Allie as mine.

She opened the door, and my jaw dropped. She wore a short black dress that had me breathless. The lacy material showed off her legs, and every last one of her curves. After a moment I pulled myself back together. "Hello there, gorgeous."

"You don't look so bad yourself." She grinned at me.

"You ready?" I reached out to touch a few of her wavy tresses. I loved when she wore her hair down.

"Definitely."

I took her hand and led her to the elevator. I couldn't take my eyes off her. I was like a school boy. She shivered. "Are you cold?"

She shook her head. "No."

"Does that mean I'm the cause of the goose bumps?"

"Maybe," she said coyly. She was so good at that. She toyed with me and left me needing more. Needing everything.

The thought of just how much she still had to offer had me grinning. "Nice."

An older couple entered the elevator one floor down. The woman smiled at us, taking in our appearance. "Celebrating something special tonight?"

"No, just a night out," Allie quickly answered.

"There is always something worth celebrating," the woman continued.

"Right," Allie replied politely. She'd switched to her I'm uncomfortable voice. "Have a nice night."

"You too." The woman smiled.

We walked out into the sticky heat of the night, headed for dinner.

I squeezed her hand. "You were wrong, you know."

"About what?"

"We are celebrating tonight."

"Oh yeah? What are we celebrating exactly?"

"We're celebrating you." I stopped short and placed a hand over her heart. "And me, and an amazing summer."

She smiled up at me. "All things worth celebrating."

We walked the rest of the way to the restaurant in near silence. I was far too nervous to come up with anything worth talking about. Instead I just enjoyed having her hand in mine and her body beside me.

We got the best table in the house at Antonie's. I'd made sure of that. I was still trying to sell Allie on the uniqueness and culture of New Orleans so the ambiance at Antoine's was perfect. I wasn't sure whether she'd ever tried French-Creole food, but Allie seemed open to almost any cuisine so I didn't worry.

The waiter approached our table shortly after we sat down. "Welcome to Antoine's. Can I get you something to drink?"

"Yes, we'll have the 1982 Chateau Mouton Rothschild." I wasn't cutting any corners. This was going to be one of the biggest nights of both of our lives.

"Nice choice, I will be back with it shortly." The waiter tried to hide his surprise. That was good if he expected a good tip.

"So you know a lot about wine?" She unwrapped her napkin.

"You could say that." I took the napkin and spread it out on her lap for her.

She didn't seem to mind the gesture. "What do you mean?"

"My family is originally from France, and we still have some vineyards in Bordeaux."

"Oh, wow. That's really cool." Allie's face matched her words. I had so much to offer her. So many things she'd get to experience for the first time.

"Yeah, it's a very beautiful area. We'll have to visit sometime." Many times.

The waiter returned with the wine, and I slowly tasted it. "Yes, perfect, thank you."

Allie watched me like she was seeing me for the first time.

After the waiter retreated, I made a toast. "To a truly amazing summer and to many more celebrations."

I watched her take her first sip. "What do you think?"

She closed her eyes. "Wow, that's really smooth."

"I thought it was perfect for tonight."

She smiled and picked up a menu.

"You don't need that." I gently removed the menu from her hands and placed it down on the table. The waiter appeared immediately.

"Are you ready to order?"

"Yes. We'll start with the huîtres a la Rockefeller and escargot la bordelaise. Then we'll both have the chateaubriand."

I waited for Allie to argue. Surely she wasn't going to let me get away with ordering for her? Surprisingly she didn't say a word. Allie was always full of surprises.

I refilled her wine glass. Either she was nervous or she really liked the wine.

She sipped the second glass slowly as we waited for the food to arrive.

Allie set her wine glass down when the waiter brought our appetizer to the table. She dug right in.

"Okay, the Oysters Rockefeller are incredible," she said between bites.

"The dish was invented here."

"Really? That's cool."

She seemed to enjoy the rest of the meal as well. I'd ordered us an entrée designed for sharing, and she appeared to enjoy the intimacy that it created. She wanted to share with me, she wanted us close. She wanted me just as much as I wanted her, and that's why I was making the right decision—for both of us.

"I have something for you." I'm sure I was sweating. Confident about my decision or not, there was still the possibility she'd refuse to accept it.

"Really? You didn't have to get me anything." She didn't cover her excitement well. She was eager for a gift.

"It's actually a family piece, but it was made for you."

"Levi... I can't take anything like that." Her face was a mix of emotions.

"Shh. Just let me enjoy giving it to you, okay?" I'd been waiting for this moment for years.

"Okay." she smiled.

I pulled out a small black box from my pocket. I wasn't taking a chance on losing that ring again. I gently opened the box, and pulled out the ring covered in rubies. I slipped the ring on her finger and my heart about stopped seeing it there.

This was right. The ring was where it belonged on her left ring finger. "Perfect." I was making the right decision I reminded myself. Allie was meant to be mine. She wanted to be mine. She would be safe with me. She'd have everything she'd ever wanted.

She absolutely glowed as she admired the ring. Then her face fell and she started to pull it off. "Levi, it's beautiful, but I can't take it."

I stilled her hand. "It looks perfect, doesn't it? Do you like it?"

"I love it. Red is my favorite color, you know."

"I know." And that was just another reminder of how right we were.

The glow was back. "Thank you. It's beautiful, and I'll treasure it."

"I'm glad."

"I can't believe the summer is almost over, it went so fast."

"Entirely too fast." I'd planned to have more time. I planned to tell her more about my life first, but I couldn't. I didn't have time for everything. I'd have to do things backward.

"So what happens now? Or when I leave?" She winced. Maybe she'd bitten her tongue.

"We'll make it work."

"You think?"

"I know." I glanced at the ring. The ring would fix everything. She'd be with me. She'd be mine.

"I guess at least we don't have to worry about airfare if you want to come to visit." She laughed lightly.

"Let's not even think about it now. Just enjoy tonight." I took her hand again, running a finger over the small stones of the ring. She'd told her parents she'd consider college in New Orleans. I really hoped she was serious. I wasn't interested in starting out our life together long distance. She needed to stay in her city.

"You're absolutely right."

"Do you want dessert?" I asked after the last of our dishes were cleared.

She paused as though she were considering it. "Maybe later."

"Good, I agree completely." I'd get her anything she wanted later, but there was something we both needed first.

I signaled for the waiter without taking my eyes off of her. I paid the check, and we headed back out onto the street.

The usual electricity between us sizzled even stronger as we walked hand in hand through Jackson Square. It was the ring. It had to be the ring.

I needed her and couldn't wait any longer. I pulled her into Pirates Alley with me and pushed her up against the bars of the railing. I moved gently as I pinned one of her arms above her head. She held onto a bar with her other hand as if to steady herself. I used my hand to pull her body toward mine.

She shivered underneath me, but her eyes never left mine.

I threw out any attempt to be gentle. I smashed my lips into hers. I held her closely, unwilling to let go as I took over her mouth again. She opened up to me. She opened up more than ever, and I knew she wanted exactly what I wanted. I used my free hand to roam her body. She wasn't shy about letting me know she liked my touch. She closed her eyes. Still, there was far too much material between us. I reluctantly broke the kiss, and she opened those beautiful green eyes.

I asked her the question with my eyes because I was unwilling to break the spell with my words. She answered the same way, and I quickly discarded my dress shirt. I returned my lips to hers before taking off. I'd never kissed her in flight before, but it was definitely an experience I would have again. It brought things to a new level of intensity.

We landed on her balcony. Without letting her go, I opened her door and moved us inside. I closed the door with my foot before leading her toward her bedroom.

My lips moved to her ear, and I gently ran my tongue over her earlobe. Her body responded as she slipped off her shoes and dropped her purse. She was ready. She was ready for me.

Never taking my eyes off her, I unzipped her dress, letting it fall to the floor. I kissed her neck as my fingers found the clasp of her bra. She disrupted my view as she pulled my shirt over my head, but it was worth it to have my bare skin against hers.

Her breasts teased me as I held her close. I tilted her head up toward me, kissing her hard on the mouth. Her perfect mouth that went with her perfect body.

She wound her arms around my neck. I intensified the kiss and picked her up. She wrapped her long legs around my waist as I carried her over to her bed.

I pulled down the comforter, placing her gently on the sheets.

She looked like an angel. Her entire body was finally on display for me, and I didn't know where to start. I'd waited so long for her. So long to see and explore every inch of the most beautiful body that I'd ever seen.

I lay down next to her, letting my eyes soak in every inch of her before my hands and mouth got their chance. Her body was even more incredible than I imagined. I cupped one of her breasts, marveling in how well it fit into my hand. Designed for me. The mate I was always meant to have. She rested her head back and closed her eyes. She was giving me full access—letting me enjoy her in any way I wanted. But I needed her to look at me. I needed to know she wanted everything I did. "Open your eyes."

"The first time you told me to do that we were hurtling through the sky."

"I do plan to give you quite the experience, Al, but this one will be a different sort of flight."

"Ok." Her lashes opened, revealing her eyes to me.

I replaced my hand with my mouth, grazing my teeth over her nipple to see how sensitive she was. I could tell she was already struggling to keep her eyes open, and I liked knowing how easily I could make her lose control.

I ran my hand down her stomach and further down. She opened up to me, letting me slip my hand between those amazing legs of hers. She was ready for me. That knowledge only turned me on more.

She took me in her hand, but before long I had to stop her. I moved over her, taking another long look at her absolutely breathtaking body. "Do you want to be mine?" I had to ask. Maybe I wasn't telling her everything, but I was still letting her choose whether or not she wanted to be with me.

"Aren't I yours already?" Her eyes were big and her breathing heavy.

"You're amazing Allie Davis." I thrust into her. She welcomed me home to the place I'd been waiting forever to find. Never in a million years had I prepared myself for the pleasure that being with her could bring.

She was so responsive, her body moving perfectly with mine as I sped things up, always careful to make sure she was comfortable. Everything felt different—I'd never experienced sex like it before, because it wasn't just sex, it was so much more.

Her breathing further picked up, and she moaned my name. Her nails dug into my back, and I groaned. Everything was so primal and perfect with her. She yelled out, before closing her eyes and rolling her head back. I shuddered, never more fulfilled than when I reached release.

I stayed on top of her, unwilling to pull out until I absolutely had to. Her body was home, it was mine. She was mine, and she was going to be mine forever.

Chapter Eleven

I never wanted to leave her bed. The night before had hands down been the best night of my life. I'd had her twice and had wanted her more, but she'd fallen asleep and there wasn't a chance I was disturbing her. Instead I contented myself by holding her and making plans. I'd need to find a new place. For the remainder of the summer we could stay in her hotel room, but afterwards I didn't want to subject her to my roommates. Pterons had incredible hearing, and I definitely didn't want her holding back when we were alone. Besides, I wanted her all to myself. I wanted showers, and half naked breakfasts, and all those things intimate couples have.

I needed to tell her. I had to explain to her that she'd just become Pteron royalty. I couldn't tell her everything at once. I needed to do it slowly. Hopefully she'd feel just as euphoric as I did.

She moaned lightly and moved in my arms. I kissed the top of her head.

She rolled over to look at me.

"Good morning, beautiful." I played with a few stands of her long brown hair that were splayed out on the pillow.

"Good morning." She smiled, confirming my hopes. There was no awkwardness, no regrets.

"You are so beautiful when you sleep."

"You watched me sleep?" She leaned up on one elbow.

"Yeah, I couldn't resist. It's not often I'm around you when you aren't being all feisty and defensive. It was nice to see you completely peaceful for a change."

"I didn't get to see you sleep… too bad." She wrapped her hand around my wrist.

"You can always watch tonight."

"Tonight? What makes you think this is ever going to happen again?"

I raised an eyebrow. "Sweetheart, you and I both know that there was nothing one time about last night."

She said nothing. Her expression said it all. She'd be lying in my arms in exactly the same position the next morning, and every morning after. I got hard just thinking about it.

"How about we just stay here all day?" I pulled her on top of me.

She rolled off of me. "Very funny. You know I have to meet Hailey for brunch." She glanced at the clock on the bed stand. "Wow, I need to meet her soon, we slept late."

"Yeah, I guess we did. You could always call and cancel." I ran a hand down her side. Her skin was so soft and smooth.

"Cancel on Hailey?" She asked incredulously.

"Okay, maybe not. She'll blame me and I'll be the one dealing with it." I laughed even though all I wanted to do was spend more time exploring her. I needed to calm down. Allie staying friends with Hailey was important for both of us.

As if sensing my less than pure thoughts she shifted away. "Besides, you have plans this morning too, don't you?"

"As if I would choose basketball with the guys over this?" I cupped her breast to make it clear exactly what I was talking about.

She bit her lip. "Well, either way I'm going, so you need to leave." She was struggling. She wanted me again.

I decided to run with it. Leaving her wanting more was just a guarantee she'd be ready later. "Fine. But we're having dinner tonight. I have something to talk to you about." Something major.

"Dinner sounds good, but what do you need to tell me?"

"Relax, it's a good thing." I touched the ruby ring. "This looks good on you."

"Thanks, I like it." She studied the ring with a smile.

"I'm glad." I enjoyed the view as she walked across her room to find some clothes. I was never going to get tired of watching her.

"If you're done staring, get dressed." She tossed my pants to me. I caught them in one hand and grudgingly got out of the bed and started dressing. "Okay, okay. Are you always this bossy in the morning?"

"I'm not exactly used to having company this early."

"Too bad, you're going to have to get used to it." I winked before picking up my shirt off the floor. I didn't mind bossy when it came from Allie. I pulled her into my arms and trailed feather light kisses from her ear down to her neck. She could be late. I needed her and considering that I had the evidence of my arousal pressed against her, she knew it too.

She pushed my chest "You better stop that, or we're never getting out of here."

"My thoughts exactly." I let my heated gaze say it all.

"Levi, come on." She was asking me to be the strong one. She wanted more, but she didn't want to disappoint a friend. Allie was principled. It was one of the things I loved about her, so I forced myself to back up. "All right, I'm going. How about I meet you around six?"

"Okay, I'll see you then." She walked me to the door.

I paused with my hand on the doorknob. "For the record, that was the best night ever. I'm going to spend the day thinking of ways to make tonight even better."

"Good-bye, Levi." She let out a sigh. My guess was she'd be thinking about the same thing.

"Bye love, don't miss me too much."

She shook her head and closed the door.

***

"What the hell has gotten into you man?" Owen tossed the basketball to the side. He'd finally realized I was way too distracted to play.

"Isn't it obvious?" Jared opened a bottle of water. "He finally fucked her."

"It wasn't fucking." I grinned. I'd never had an experience I felt like kissing and telling about. This one I was ready to shout from the rooftops.

"Yeah?" Owen asked with suddenly more interest. "How was it?"

"Perfect. She's absolutely perfect."

"She does have a great body." Jared downed the rest of his water.

"A body that isn't yours to look at."

"I'm not interested in touching the girl, but you can't stop me from looking."

"She's mine. I can stop you from doing anything."

"Yours? Staking a claim are you?" Jared loved pushing my buttons. If he was looking for a fight though, he wasn't going to get it. I was in way too good of a mood.

"She's been mine since the moment I laid eyes on her." Now that she was wearing my ring on her finger I could be as confident as I wanted. She was mine, and no one could take her from me.

My phone rang from where I'd left it with my stuff. I grabbed it, hoping it was Allie telling me she couldn't wait to see me. It was Hailey. Almost as important. I picked up. "Hey."

"You fucking asshole!"

I held the phone away from my ear. Hailey was loud even when she wasn't yelling. "Uh, Allie wasn't that late, was she?" I smiled to myself knowing why she wasn't on time.

"Are you guys still at the gym?"

"Yes."

"I'm on my way."

"Is Allie coming too?" I hoped she was. I couldn't wait to taste those lips again.

"No. She's not." Hailey hung up.

"What was that about?" Owen asked worriedly. Very few people could get away with cursing me out without severe consequences. Being Allie's friend had bought Hailey some slack.

Five minutes later Hailey stormed into the gym. She walked right over and slapped me across the face. "I knew you were stupid, but this stupid?"

I touched my cheek. "What are you talking about?"

"Don't play dumb." She glared at me. Did Hailey know? Had she noticed the ring?

"What did you just do, Hailey?" Owen pulled her away from me. "You hit Levi?"

"He deserves it. After what he did to her. After what he did to all of us." She seethed.

"What is she talking about?" Owen dropped his sister's arm and looked at me. "You look upset. Which means something she's saying is true."

"You didn't." Jared strode over. "Please tell me last night was just a fuck."

"I did."

"What are you talking about?" Owen stared blankly. Either he hadn't pieced it together or he was afraid to accept it.

"I gave her the ring. I had to. She was going to leave in a few weeks, and we'd waited so long already. I figured I might as well give her the ring the first time to make it more special."

Understanding crossed Owen's face. "You gave her the ring and slept with her? You consummated it? She's your mate?"

"Yes, and I don't regret it." I wasn't going to listen to their lectures. "She's the one."

"You didn't tell her anything. How? How could you?" I'd never heard Hailey at a loss for words before.

"Wait? You didn't tell her what the ring meant?" Jared asked. "You just gave the girl a royal ring and took her to bed?" Jared's mouth fell open. "That's the kind of asshole move I'd pull. Not you."

"I'm going to tell her tonight. She's happy with me. It's all going to work out."

"I wouldn't wait until tonight." Hailey glanced at me guiltily. "I'd probably go to her hotel. She isn't answering her phone."

"Why wouldn't she be? Oh no." Complete and utter panic filled me. "You didn't. You didn't tell her, did you?"

"What was I supposed to do?"

"Fuck." I grabbed my wallet and keys. "I'm going to see her."

Chapter Twelve

Her hotel room was empty. Her stuff was still there, which put me slightly at ease, but her car wasn't in the garage or parked nearby, and from what I could tell she hadn't come back after her brunch with Hailey.

I turned to Jared. "Track down her car. She's probably near it." Having the son of the head of security around came in handy sometimes.

"You put a tracker on it? You put a tracker on her car?" Hailey got up in my face.

I stepped around her. "Yes, after the attempted carjacking. We had to make sure Allie stayed safe."

I paced her room, trying to handle the overwhelming fear that Allie hated me and that something could have happened to her. When we got her back, and it was when and not if, I was never letting her out of my sight. She'd have to forgive me. She had no choice. She was wearing my ring.

Jared pocketed his phone. "Found the car. I'm going in."

"Just give me the coordinates. I'm going."

"I don't think that's such a good idea." Owen swallowed hard. "She's angry with you. What if she runs away and does something stupid?"

"I hate to agree with Owen, but I do." Hailey smiled for the first time since I'd seen her that morning. "Jared's good. He'll get to her and bring her back. Then we figure out what happens next."

"Where is the car?" I didn't have to listen to any of them, and I wouldn't. I needed to get Allie back.

"Levi…" Hailey said softly.

"Before I leave I want intel. Where is she? What locals do we have there?"

"It's Tennessee. Kind of the middle of nowhere. You want to call someone in?"

Tennessee? Had she been driving back to New York? "Yes, but we need to be quiet." I didn't need to tell my friends why. If my dad found out she'd left, we'd have an even more serious problem on our hands.

Jared had an update moments later. They'd found the car and her purse in a Dairy Queen parking lot, but no Allie.

"What do you mean her purse was just in the parking lot?" My body tensed.

Jared ran a hand through his hair nervously. "Her car is in the lot and her purse is sitting there."

"Let's go." I'd start at the parking lot and work from there.

"No." Jared put a hand on my arm. "I will."

"But she hates you."

"Not as much as she probably hates you. Trust me on this." His eyes bore into mine.

I stepped toward him. "You can't tell me what to do."

"No, but I can tell you to use reason."

A light knock on the door had us all turning. I pulled it open, half hoping and expecting Allie to suddenly be back.

"What did you do, Levi?" Mom walked into the room.

"What are you doing here?"

"Hailey suggested I show up. Something to do with you messing something major up."

Jared shook his head. "We don't have time for this. I'm going up." I'd never seen Jared so single-minded on something that wasn't about him. I assumed he wanted to prove his worth.

I exhaled sharply. "I picked my mate, and she's missing."

"She's missing?" Mom glanced at me, completely skimming over the picking a mate part.

"Levi didn't tell her what the ring meant. I let it slip and she ran." Hailey looked down at the ground.

"And Jared knows where she is?"

"Dad and I had a tracker put on her car."

"Your father knew about her before me?" The hurt in my mom's eyes was undeniable, but I couldn't fix that yet.

"He didn't find out from me, and you can meet her first." Maybe that would smooth things over. "I'm going to get her."

Mom shook her head. "No."

"Why not?" Was my own mother turning against me?

"Do you want everyone to find out what happened? If word gets out that we've lost your mate... you know what that would mean."

"I don't care. I need to be the one to get her." I yanked Jared's phone from his hand and read the coordinates. I'm going.

Owen and Jared each grabbed one of my arms. "No." they said in unison.

Jared tightened his hold. "Think about it, man. Don't make things worse. You can trust me to bring her back to you."

"Levi, hon." Mom looked me in the eyes. "We're going to get her back. Then you're going to introduce us, and we're going to fix everything."

But what if we couldn't? What if she was really gone? They were arguing what I already knew was the truth. Losing my mate meant losing the crown, and if anyone found out it could set off serious panic.

"The longer you keep me here the longer until she's back with you. Calm down so I can take care of this." Jared knew how my mind worked.

"Okay." I pushed off my friends. "I'll stay back, but not for long. I want constant updates."

"I'll have her back here soon." Jared walked to the door. "I'll find a discrete place to fly from." He was only saying that for the benefit of my mother. Jared and discrete didn't usually go together. Hopefully he wouldn't cause more trouble.

***

I didn't leave the hotel for hours. I could have waited for news anywhere, but somehow being in the same building she'd been staying in made her feel closer. Besides, my mother, Owen, and Hailey wouldn't have let me leave even if I'd tried. They were afraid I'd fly up and cause an even bigger problem.

Waiting around for news was torture. I felt helpless and useless. All I wanted to do was get her back. There had to be something I could do.

The call came from an associate in the mountains. Jared was on his way back. Hailey leaned in close. "Don't make this any harder than it needs to be."

"I need to see her. I need to make sure she's okay."

"I don't know if she even wants to see me..." Hailey had bit her lip so hard she was bleeding. If I hadn't been so worried about Allie I might have been concerned about the toll on Hailey. But Allie's safety came first. I needed to know she was okay.

"I can't do this. You can't make me stay away."

Mom patted my arm. "It's not forever. Just let the dust settle."

"The dust had better settle fast."

"Believe it or not I agree with you." Hailey sighed and stalked out of the room.

Chapter Thirteen

I waited for her in front of the corner coffee shop. After a while, I stopped watching for her to show up. I was only messing with myself more. Owen and Hailey were going to take care of getting her to me. The rest was in my hands. I was lucky I was even getting this chance. It sounded like Hailey had had to twist her arm. I'd use my opportunity well. I needed to fix this.

The Blackwells' hadn't gotten her, but she'd still spent time at the hands of cougar shifters who had no business looking at her, let alone hurting her. Just thinking about the situation made me angry, and I couldn't afford that. I needed to stay calm if I was going to change her mind about staying with me. Staying wasn't just about being with me and keeping the crown, it was also about her safety. I'd never let anything happen to Allie again.

"Hey man," Owen called out. He was walking right next to Allie. Hailey was on her other side. A territorial side in me wanted to pull her away from him, but I knew he was only helping me.

Allie and I locked eyes. The emotion in hers was clear as day. Deep down she still wanted me, still cared, but the rest of her face was all anger.

I stepped toward her, reaching out a hand. She slunk back, so I dropped my arm. We stood there watching each other for a moment before I couldn't wait any longer. I pulled her into my arms. "I'm so glad you're safe."

She whimpered quietly and pulled away. Had I made her this sad? Had something more happened?

"Okay, so we're going to get going…" Hailey said trailing off. "Come on, Owen."

"Oh yeah. Bye," Owen said.

The brother and sister duo disappeared down the street.

"You want to go inside?" I asked, needing to make sure she didn't bolt.

"Sure." She'd said yes, but there wasn't much enthusiasm in her voice. She wasn't thrilled to see me.

I held open the door, and she headed straight for the counter. "One large coffee."

"Make that two." I handed a credit card to the barista. She could order on her own to make a point, but that didn't mean I wasn't going to make my point by paying.

She added her own sweetener to her coffee and took a seat at a table. I wished she'd let me do it for her. I wanted to do everything for her. I would have done anything to make things up to her.

I sat down at the table across from her. I wanted to sit next to her, but I needed to give her space.

She kept her eyes fixed on her coffee.

"If it changes anything, I didn't mean to upset you."

Her head snapped up. "What?"

"I didn't want to hurt you." I reached my hand across the table, desperate to touch her, but she jerked her hand away.

"Then what did you want exactly?" Her voice was cold, and that hurt nearly as much as her refusal to touch me.

"You." I looked right into her eyes. She needed to know I did everything for us. I needed her by my side, and it was where she belonged.

"Clever, very clever."

"It's the truth. You asked why I did it and that's the honest answer. I did it because I wanted you."

"What part of wanting me required you to trick me into entering into some weird relationship?"

"Weird relationship? Is that what you think this is?" I still didn't know how much Hailey had told her.

"What am I supposed to think it is?"

"There is nothing weird about it, most girls would be happy to find out they've become a princess." At least I thought they would. I was giving her everything. She'd never want for anything in her life. She was from some money, but her dad's company was nothing compared to what being a Laurent meant for her.

"I guess I'm not like most girls. And what is with all this princess talk? When were you going to tell me you were the future king or whatever it is they call you exactly?"

"It didn't seem important before… and I didn't want to scare you off." Obviously my decision to hold back that information back fired.

She laughed dryly. "Well, you did a pretty good job with that."

"It wasn't supposed to be like this."

"No? What was it supposed to be like? Am I supposed to fawn at your feet thanking you for picking me? Dream on."

"Damn it, don't be so difficult. You were there that night. We work so well together. It's amazing. Can't that be enough?" My heart ached. She needed to understand. She needed to accept how perfect we were for each other.

"You have that much confidence in your sexual prowess to think that means anything?"

"I am not talking about me, I'm talking about us."

"There is no *us*. Whatever chance we had is gone. You tricked me, lied to me, used me, and pretty much did anything you possibly could to destroy us." She pulled her hands onto her lap. "You're the reason I was kidnapped and nearly raped. It's your fault." She looked down at her hands

My chest clenched, my body tensed, and I was ready to transform. Nearly raped? "I am so sorry. Words can't even describe it. The thought of those brutes touching you…" I gripped the table, my knuckles turning white. "I promise you they will never bother you or anyone else again." They'd never be doing anything again. I scooted my chair closer to her. "Please, give me a chance to make it up to you." I didn't hold back. I pleaded. I needed her to understand.

She looked up at me through tear rimmed eyes. "The only thing I want is an explanation. Why me? Why in the world did you pick me? You hardly know me."

Now that was a weighted question. How could I possibly put my feelings into adequate words? "I've never felt this way about anyone before. Usually I get tired of a girl after a few days, but you? I'll never get tired of you. You challenge me, and it only makes me want you more. I know you feel it too. Don't bother denying it. The physical pull between us is undeniable."

"That's what this is all about? You're physically attracted to me? I still don't see how that makes me different."

"Doesn't the thought of being together excite you at all? You seemed so interested in my world, so caught up in it. Can't that be enough for now?"

She glanced around at several onlookers staring and lowered her voice. "Levi, are you even listening to me? Do you really expect me to forgive you for what you put me through? You make it sound like you stood me up."

"I'm sorry baby, I'm sorry. You were only kidnapped because you ran off. I didn't expect you to do that. I already planned to explain more over dinner. Remember, I told you I had something important to tell you." I leaned over the table.

"Don't you ever call me baby. Do you hear me? Never!" Her expression was equal parts anger and fear.

I would kill those stupid cougars, but first I had to make things right with her. "Okay. I won't. I'm sorry." I picked up one of her hands, looking at the cuts and bruises on her wrist. She pulled her hand back. "I'm so sorry."

She sighed. "Didn't you think I'd try to take the ring off?"

I shrugged. I hadn't thought that far ahead. I planned on just telling her that night. I was blinded by the need to make her stay. "I never really thought about it."

"Exactly!" She stood up, nearly knocking over her chair. "You didn't think and look where it got us."

I followed after her as she hurried outside.

"Wait up!" I took her arm and pulled her toward me.

"Let go of me!"

"You don't understand how important this is. You can't just walk away from me. You have to be with me now."

"I don't have to do anything."

"Give me a chance to explain more, to show you."

"I gave you that chance inside." She gestured to the door we just walked through.

"Let me show you more of my people, introduce you, make you see how important you are."

"Why would I do that?"

"Because you're a good person. Because even if you hate me, you don't hate Hailey and you sure as hell don't hate the city of New Orleans."

"Why would being together affect New Orleans?"

"It means everything. Without you, my family's reign ends and the headquarters likely moves—taking everything with it. Do you really want to see New Orleans robbed of more? Like Katrina wasn't enough."

"Shut up!" She yelled. "Don't compare me leaving to a hurricane!"

"There is so much you don't understand. New Orleans needs us. Please let me show you. If you still don't want anything to do with us afterward, we'll figure something else out, but at least give me one night to prove it to you." I didn't want to bring up her safety. I'd let someone else do that. The thought of seeing any more fear on that beautiful face of hers made me want to transform.

"One night?"

"Yes. Just one night." I needed at least that. I needed to make her understand how important she was.

"Fine. One night and then you find a way to let me leave."

I sighed with relief. I had a shot. "Good."

We walked the rest of the way back to the hotel in silence. She wouldn't let me help her even though I could tell she was in pain. I felt helpless. Allie made me feel more helpless than I'd ever felt in my life.

We reached the hotel, and I held open the door for her. She walked right in. I called after her. "I'll see you soon. I'll have Hailey give you all the details."

"Details?" She stopped walking, and I caught up. "What kind of night is this?"

I smiled. "Just wait and see. All I'll tell you is that it's a party." I kissed her on the cheek before walking away.

***

My next stop wasn't one I was looking forward to. I had to tell my dad I'd officially taken her as my mate. The problem was I'd only be able to give him half the details. Somehow I didn't think that would go over well. Thankfully my mom was with me when I stepped into my dad's home office. Thankfully, Mom seemed to be completely over her annoyance at me.

"It's done? She's wearing your ring?" Dad was opening a bottle of whiskey before I even stopped speaking.

"Yes. Allie is wearing my ring." That much was true.

"Wonderful. I'm proud of you, Levi. When's the wedding going to be?"

I glanced at my mom, hoping she could help me out. "Allie's young, Robert. Only eighteen."

My father quickly brushed off the concern. "So? That's a legal age to marry."

"Yes, but think of her parents. Her father may not be comfortable with it."

"I'll talk to the man."

"She's agreed to our party though. We can just hold off on the human events." At least I had that to offer him.

"Good enough for now. When do I meet the girl?"

"At the engagement party later this week."

"Later this week? Perfect. She must be lovely if she was able to get you to settle down." Dad gave me a knowing look.

"She's perfect. The most beautiful girl I've ever met. She's stubborn and strong headed, but I love that about her."

"Sounds like you met your match."

"I have."

"Is that all?" Leave it to my father to want more than just the most monumental news of my lifetime. I'd given her the ring. For all he knew, everything was settled. Did he know more? The thought froze my blood. Allie and I would both be in serious trouble if that was the case.

"That's all." I took his opening and left the office. I wasn't sure if I could handle any real questioning.

Mom caught up with me just as I walked outside. "We need to get her to agree."

"I know." I smiled tersely before heading back home.

Chapter Fourteen

Allie looked heavenly in the red dress my mother had made for her. She looked gorgeous in everything, but seeing her in my family's color while everyone else wore black and white set me on fire.

Everyone noticed her. The chatter of the crowd died down as she walked in. I set aside my glass of wine and left a business associate mid-sentence as I made my way across the room to her. "You look amazing."

"Thank you." She took in my appearance. Hopefully she liked the way I looked in a black tux. "Was the red dress really necessary?"

"Absolutely. Red is definitely your color by the way."

"You can give it up, Levi. Flattery isn't going to get you anywhere."

I shrugged. I saw the way her face brightened. Flattery helped. She cared about my approval whether she admitted it or not. "I'm just speaking the truth. Did you have any trouble getting here? The car came on time and everything?"

"Everything was fine," she said distantly.

"I'm sorry I couldn't bring you myself."

"Hailey explained why *she* couldn't come get me." She spoke quietly, but the words still hit home. I'd have picked her up myself if I could have, but I had to do things by the books or someone would have figured out that not everything was as it seemed.

"I'm glad you're here."

"It's beautiful."

"Not as beautiful as you." Nothing in the world was as beautiful as her.

"Is Hailey here?" She gazed out at the crowd. "Wait, isn't that the Governor of Louisiana?"

"Yeah, that's Bobby," I said nonchalantly. "Remind me to introduce you later."

"Is that Hailey over there?" Allie looked across the room. I barely recognized Hailey with her elaborate up do. Whether Owen liked it or not, she definitely wasn't a little kid anymore.

"We can go talk to her in a minute. Do you mind if we talk to my parents first?"

She nodded.

I took her arm and led her over to my parents. She'd already met my mom, but the big introduction would be to my father. I'd been told I looked like a younger version of him. I suppose aside from his gray hair we did look alike.

"Allie, you look breathtaking." My mother embraced her warmly. At least I could count on my mom to be helpful.

"Thank you, Helen. You look wonderful as well." Allie smiled. She seemed perfectly at ease with the situation, and I wondered how much of it was an act.

My father broke into a broad smile when he noticed her. "Ah, Allison, my son didn't exaggerate your beauty after all."

Allie wrinkled up her nose before her face returned to normal. My guess was it had to do with his use of her full name. I had to smile at that. "It's nice to meet you, Mr. Laurent."

"It's just Robert. I suppose you could also call me Dad if you wanted, since you'll be my daughter-in-law soon." He beamed.

Allie looked panicked. I hadn't exactly mentioned that my father didn't know the truth. I hoped she would just go along with it. "I think I'll use Robert."

"Fair enough. Levi tells me you two aren't going to be rushing into a formal wedding. I understand your father's concern with how young you are, but I'd be happy to talk to him for you. I look forward to meeting him sometime soon."

Allie fidgeted uncomfortably. "It was wonderful to meet you, but Levi, would you mind stepping outside with me for a moment? I could use some fresh air."

"Of course, sweetheart." I took her hand. I needed to get her away from my dad before she lost it on me.

"We'll be right back," I reassured my father.

We walked away from the tent, and I had to resist the urge to swoop her up in my arms. She seemed to be in some pain again.

She spun around. "What the heck, Levi? Your dad thinks I've agreed to marry you?"

"Look, I know you're mad, but with my dad there was no choice. He would have gone crazy if I told him the truth, and trust me it wouldn't have helped you at all."

"What are you talking about? All it would mean is us not playing this little game here. Like we're fooling anyone."

"Lower your voice. Seriously, if my dad finds out the truth we're both in trouble." She didn't want to know what my dad was like when he got angry.

"What's he going to do to me?"

"My dad is in charge of the entire paranormal community, and you doubt he could do something to you?" The ring couldn't be undone. She had to be my mate. He'd find a way to make her stay whether she wanted to or not.

"I'm just a human. He can't hurt me."

"First of all, you are not just a human. You are my mate. Big difference, and he could force you to marry me tonight if he wanted to."

"What are you talking about?" She shivered. She needed to be frightened of my Dad. I'd do everything to protect her, but my dad wasn't someone to mess with.

"Like I said my dad has his ways. Let's stop this. You promised to give tonight a chance. Please, won't you at least try?"

"Okay."

"Are you ready to go back in?"

"Sure."

We walked back into the tent to the sound of clinking as several people tried to silence the crowd. My father strode purposely to the center of the dance floor.

"Thank you everyone for being with us tonight. It isn't often that we have the pleasure of welcoming so many members of the community to our home, and we are so thankful that you were able to join us on this happy occasion. Many of you probably thought this day would never come." My father paused as the crowd laughed politely. They would have laughed no matter how corny his lines were.

"I am well aware of my son's reputation with women, but it seems he has met his match. I have never seen Levi so happy or focused, and I know that we can expect great things from him as he formally takes his position next year. On that note, it's my pleasure to introduce you to Allison Davis, Levi's beautiful mate."

I steered Allie over to my Dad. She leaned into my side, seemingly happy to let me take the lead. "Thank you father. You're right. I have met my match, and she's my match in every sense of the word. I have no doubt you will all learn to adore her as much as I do. Our community is new to her, but I am sure she will make a seamless transition. Now sweetheart, will you give me this dance?"

She nodded.

A quartet struck up a beautiful ballad and loud applause filled the tent as I led her onto the dance floor. I took a slight bow and gestured for her to do the same. I watched my beautiful mate as I easily led us in a waltz. Her body moved comfortably with mine. Despite her words, I knew how natural she felt at my side.

The song came to an end, but the quartet started another slow tune without a break.

Taking advantage of the slower music, I leaned in. "Al, I'm sorry. I'd do anything to erase what happened to you. I messed up. I know I did, but I also know that there is something real between us."

"I don't see how you expect me to believe that."

"Please. It's true. We have to at least give this a chance," I pleaded. I was running out of time to convince her.

"So, what, I throw away all my plans?"

"Defer Princeton until the spring. One semester at Tulane won't hurt. You'll probably like it. We can make sure you're roommates with Hailey and everything." I'd do whatever it took to make her comfortable. She'd love Tulane. I just knew it.

She hesitated with her answer and I waited with baited breath. "If I agree, it's only for a semester."

"So you'll give us a chance?" My heart soared.

"This isn't about you and me. This is about New Orleans and keeping myself and my family safe. I'll stay, but you need to accept that we're not really together."

I pulled her tight against my chest. I'd change her mind. I just needed time. "I love you. I have never felt this way before, and the thought of losing you scares me."

"And that's supposed to make everything better?" She bristled. "You love me? It doesn't matter anyway."

"Why not?"

"Because I don't love you."

Her words hit me like a slap across the face, but the sting faded as I gazed into those green eyes. She didn't mean it. She loved me just as I loved her. No matter what she said now, I'd change her mind. I'd do anything to make her happy, anything to make her stay. Allie and I belonged together, and no matter what it took, she'd be mine forever.

The Royal Wedding

Levi

Watching Allie walk down the aisle changed me. Bound already or not, there was something incredible about seeing her dressed in a white wedding gown with her eyes fixed right on me. There was so much emotion in those green eyes of hers. It's like she was saying more with her eyes than she could ever say with words, and I hoped my eyes were doing the same thing. I'd been in love with Allie since the moment I first held her in my arms. My feelings for her were so intense they scared me, and it takes a lot for anything to do that.

The sun was high in the sky, and it casted shadows across the pristine sand. The beach wedding had been Allie's idea, and I couldn't think of anything more perfect.

She glided on her father's arm in front of over fifty people, but it might as well have just been us. She tried to keep a serious face, but the closer she got to me, the more her lips curled up until she was nearly grinning. I loved having that effect on her. I loved knowing that I could make her happy in a way that no one else could.

Allie

Levi. All I could see and focus on was his handsome face, and those darn blue-gray eyes watching me with an intensity and love so strong I could physically feel it. Only my father's hold kept me from rushing down the aisle. Tradition or not, I just wanted to be in his arms.

I fought down tears. I hadn't sat through an hour of makeup application to ruin it before I reached Levi's side. I needed to hold it together a little bit longer.

I took small steps as a cello and flute played *A Variation on a Theme*. I'd selected the song months before, but hearing it only made me more emotional. Even with the music I could hear the sounds of the waves gently crashing against the shore.

I was vaguely aware of our guests sitting on either side of the aisle, but I couldn't tear my eyes from Levi—the man who'd stolen my heart without me knowing it. I'd fought my feelings for him, but I'd never had a chance of staying away. Levi and I were made for each other. I had no doubt about that.

Finally, what felt like ages later, I reached the front, and Levi held my hands in his. I briefly glanced at my mom and bridesmaids before my eyes locked on Levi's again.

Levi

I couldn't cry. Shedding tears wasn't an option, so I held them back. If I wasn't mistaken, my bride was doing the same thing. She held on to my hands like her life depended on it, but she didn't need to worry. I'd have never let her fall. I'd always be there to catch her.

My dad's advisor officiated. He was kind of like an uncle to me, and his father had married my parents. I'm not the biggest on traditions, but I liked that we were continuing that one.

I barely heard the words being spoken. I was too busy studying every little detail about Allie's appearance. She was wearing more makeup than usual, but it was still natural, and her hair was wavy and fell perfectly down her back.

"And now the couple will share the vows they've written."

The personal vows had been my idea, the one deviation from the more traditional ceremony.

I started, staring into Allie's eyes as I held her hands. "Allie Davis, you are my everything. I fell for you the first moment I saw you, and nothing could have kept me away. You make me a better man, and I can't imagine where I'd be without you at my side. I know that the road here wasn't always the easiest, but I don't regret a second of the journey." I paused to brush a few tears off Allie's cheek. "I waited years to find you, and I would have spent a lifetime searching. I'd give anything to protect you, and I will love you for every single moment of my life."

Allie sniffled and dabbed her eyes. She squeezed my hand, trying to compose herself before she started with her vows. "Levi Laurent, you make my world go round. Nothing is ever better, sweeter, or more enjoyable than the time I spend with you. You make me stronger, and I know I can face anything as long as we're together. Although I fought my feelings for you at first, I'll never fight them again. I love you with every bit of my heart, and I promise to love you until my last breath."

For a moment I couldn't breathe. I was so overcome with emotion, that I didn't know which way was up. The officiant continued with the ceremony as I tried to pull myself together. I knew I was the luckiest man alive.

"Do you Leviathan Laurent take Allison Davis as your lawfully wedded wife?" The word wife got my attention. The yes slipped from my lips immediately.

"Do you Allison Davis take Leviathan Laurent as your lawfully wedded husband?"

I waited for the yes so I could kiss her.

"Let me think about that." She smiled, pretending to mull it over.

I smiled back. I knew she was only joking.

She stepped even closer to me. "Ok. I do."

"With the power—"

I didn't let him finish. I had Allie in my arms and my lips on hers within seconds. She tasted as sweet and irresistible as always, and I didn't care that we had an audience. Officially, in every way, shape, or form, Allie and I were together forever.

Allie

The term giddy took on new meaning as we walked into the reception. We were so excited to celebrate with our guests that we didn't even wait to be announced. We were married. I was Mrs. Levi Laurent, and I couldn't have been happier.

I glided around the room on Levi's arm unable to stop smiling. My face was starting to hurt, but I didn't care. Nothing could spoil my mood.

Levi was all about grand gestures. When he refused to tell me what our first dance song would be I didn't fight him. I figured there was a reason for his secrecy.

I didn't recognize the song, but it felt right, it felt perfect. Starting off slow with just piano and cello, it quickly picked up when the rest of the band kicked in.

"Did you have this song made for us?" I asked as we danced around the room.

"You mean the world to me Allie, and I wanted a song that summed that up. Nothing else fit."

I smiled and closed my eyes. I knew Levi would lead me.

All too soon the song ended, and Levi led me over to our sweethearts table. I spent most of the night dancing on Levi's arm, but I made time to visit with every one of our guests. I cried some serious tears at Hailey's toast, and my eyes definitely weren't dry when my dad made his.

Levi

The reception was fun, but all I wanted to do was get Allie alone. I had a two week honeymoon planned on our own private island. After all the craziness we'd had to go through, Allie deserved my undivided attention, and hell I deserved hers. Just the thought of what that attention would feel like had me hard. I took a deep breath. We had way too much family around to even think about that.

Allie

Saying goodbye to our guests was harder than I expected. The past year of my life had been a crazy one, and I knew I wouldn't have made it without the help of my family and friends. I didn't bother holding back the tears when I hugged my mom goodbye next to where our plane sat on the small runway. I hated keeping secrets from her, and I hoped that one day I'd be able to tell her the truth about everything. Saying goodbye to Jared was surprisingly emotional too. Considering the way our relationship started, I still couldn't believe we'd become such good friends.

"You doing okay?" Levi put an arm around me as the plane took off.

"I'm fine, great really. I'm just emotional."

He turned to look at me. "The good kind of emotional, right?"

I rested my head against his chest. "Of course. I think I just surprised myself with how hard today hit me."

"It hit me hard too." He rubbed small circles on my back. For some reason, his admission made me feel better. If Levi was emotional, then it was completely normal for me to be too.

"Are you ready to tell me where you're taking me?"

"You've waited this long, and now you want me to ruin the surprise?" He teased.

"Can you at least tell me how long it's going to take to get there?"

"In other words you want to know if you have time to take a nap?"

"How do you know me this well?"

"It's a gift." He kissed my forehead. "And you might as well nap, babe, it's not like you'll be getting any sleep tonight."

I sighed, snuggling into him more. "Why did you have to say that? Now how am I supposed to sleep?"

"I guess you won't be." He unbuckled my seatbelt and pulled me onto his lap so I was straddling him. I didn't have much room for my legs, but I didn't particularly care. Levi's lap was a favorite place of mine.

"I'm not having sex with you on your plane, Levi."

"Who said anything about sex? Can't a man just want to stare longingly into his wife's eyes?"

I laughed. "You really like saying that, don't you?"

"Don't you like calling me your husband?"

"I haven't tried it yet."

"What are you waiting for?" He ran his hands up and down my bare arms. As usual, his touch sent shivers through me.

"I love my husband."

"Yeah? That's convenient, isn't it?"

I laughed and slipped one hand underneath the bottom of his t-shirt. "Two whole weeks alone together, do you think we'll still like each other by the end?"

"I could spend eternity alone with you, Al."

"Al? You haven't called me that in a while."

"I know." He rested his hands on my hips. "I just felt like using it."

"My name's Allie Laurent now."

"Really?" He ran a finger over my hip, making me wish the fabric from my sundress wasn't in the way. At least I'd changed out of my wedding gown.

"I wanted to make sure you knew."

"I know. I've considered it to be your name for a while now."

"I think it has a great ring to it."

"Of course it does. It was the name you were born to have."

"Really? What if I'd asked you to take my last name?"

"Your last name doesn't come with a crown, babe."

"Good point." I leaned forward and brushed my lips against his. "Despite the stresses, I kind of like being queen."

"That's a good thing, because you're going to be my queen forever."

Levi

At the last minute I decided to forego the blindfold. Knowing Allie she'd read into it and think it was something kinky, and that definitely wasn't the case. The next two weeks were about romance, and I wanted to start it off right.

I had several locations to choose from, but a private island in the South Pacific was a no brainer. Whether I liked it or not, Allie and I lived a public life. I was going to take advantage of any alone time I could get.

I wrapped my hand around hers as we walked toward our cottage. The small wooden house was located over the crystal clear water of the Pacific. I knew Allie would appreciate the simple house. If we wanted luxury we'd have gone back to our mansion. I knew all she cared about was hot water and a working kitchen. Other than that we were steering clear of technology.

We walked past the large hammock and to the front door.

"I love it." She walked right in as soon as I unlocked the door. She didn't drop my hand, so I let her pull me in after her. I left the door open. I wanted to leave the cottage as open to the elements as possible. Allie loved listening to the waves, and she was going to get to do that every second of our trip.

"Do I get a tour?" She used her free hand to tug on my belt loop.

I let her pull me toward her. "That depends."

"The tour can start and end in the bedroom." She smiled that sexy, come get me smile that made me lose control.

"I think that can be arranged." I waited until she'd turned back around before I picked her up by the waist.

She squealed, and I threw her over my shoulder. "You said you only wanted a tour of the bedroom, no reason to waste any time."

I set her down just inside the simple bedroom. I took a second to open up the curtains, giving us a view of the water. I returned to Allie's side and watched as her eyes settled on the bed. "Are you really going to leave me waiting?"

I settled my hands on her hips. "Do I ever leave you waiting?"

"No… at least not in a bad way."

I reached up and untied the halter tie of her sundress. The top fell away, revealing what I already knew. She wasn't wearing a bra underneath. I held myself back. I wanted to see all of my bride before enjoying her. We'd been together more times than I could count, but somehow this felt different. She was Allie Laurent now, and I wanted to remember every second of the first time I made love to her as her husband.

I pulled her dress down over her hips, letting it fall into a satisfying heap on the floor around her feet. She didn't move to step out of it. I took a moment to admire her standing there in just a silky red pair of panties. She knew how to drive me wild.

She started on the buttons of my dress shirt, taking each one excruciatingly slow. I guess I was getting a taste of my own medicine. After discarding my shirt she slipped her hands under my t-shirt and pulled it over my head.

She reached for my belt, but I stopped her. "I want to finish undressing you first." I moved to my knees and used my teeth to lower the satin fabric off of her body. She let out a small moan as I brushed my lips against her on the way down.

She barely let me stand up before going to work on my belt again. She eased my pants and boxers down in one motion, wasting no time before taking me in her hand.

I groaned. "You kill me, babe."

"What do you think you do to me?"

Instead of answering I led her over to the bed. I pulled back the covers, she always liked it better on the sheets.

She lay down, a vision of lightly sun-kissed skin and brown hair against the red sheets. I lay down next to her, letting my lips begin a decent from her neck on down. She moaned, leaning her head back to give me better access. I took her breasts in my hands, still amazed at how perfectly they fit into my palms. Everything about Allie fit me perfectly. She moaned again, clearly enjoying the sensation of my touch. I was enjoying her touch just as much. I let my lips continue their descent down as my hand found its way between those long legs of hers. She opened up for me at the same time that she pulled my head back up to meet her own. Her lips crushed into mine, and I made my way into her mouth.

"I want you," Allie whispered, driving her hips into me to give me the hint.

"I know that, babe. The question is, are you ready for me?"

"Don't you already know the answer?" She breathed the words, clearly trying to stay in control.

"That doesn't mean I don't want to hear it."

"I'm ready for you. I want you, and I need you, now." She pushed her hips against me again, and I was done playing around.

I moved over her, giving her a second to realize she was getting exactly what she asked for. "I love you."

"I love you too."

I thrust into her, finding her as ready as I knew she'd be. I moved deeper, but kept things gentle. We had two weeks to devour each other's bodies. Tonight was for making love. Allie Davis was everything to me, and I couldn't wait to spend the rest of our lives together.

The Pteron story continues in the Empire Chronicles! Keep reading for a preview of *Soar* (The Empire Chronicles #1). Also look for *Dire* (The Dire Wolves Chronicles #1) releasing September 2014!

www.AlyssaRoseIvy.com
www.facebook.com/AlyssaRoseIvy
twitter.com/AlyssaRoseIvy
AlyssaRoseIvy@gmail.com

To stay up to date on Alyssa's new releases, join her mailing list: http://eepurl.com/ktlSj

Soar

the
empire chronicles

ALYSSA ROSE IVY

Chapter One
Casey

Glowing Eyes. In the chaos of the moment, the only thing I could focus on were the yellow eyes that followed my every move. They were eerie and seemed more at home on an animatronic creation than on the living, breathing animal that had me cornered in the alley. I knew I was stuck, but I didn't think about death. It wasn't an option because I wasn't ready for it. Realistic or not, I was a firm believer that we make our own destiny.

I stepped back, convinced that if I walked backward slowly enough, I'd escape. I silently cursed Eric for making me throw out the trash after my shift. He was such an ass of an assistant manager.

At first, the wolf didn't move—at least I thought it was a wolf, although it seemed two sizes too big. As strange as it should have been to see a giant wolf in an alley, I'd seen far stranger in my nine months of living in New York City.

"Easy boy," I said in a half whisper, more for myself than for the beast now taking slow, deliberate steps toward me.

All of a sudden, he lunged. Gray fur moved in a blur as I blocked my face the best I could in the spilt second I had. A whimper rang out, and I lowered my arms when the contact never came.

The gray wolf slowly limped out of the alley. I searched for an explanation as I struggled to regain my breath and vaguely saw another figure disappear into the distance. He could have been any man, except that in my adrenaline-rich state, I could have sworn he had wings.

My head started to spin, and I reached out for something to hold onto. Then everything went black.

***

"Hey, Bates! Are you okay?"

I forced my eyes open, confused about the cause of my killer headache and the fogginess permeating my head.

"Casey?" Eric bent down next to me with some legitimate concern on his face. "Are you all right?"

"How long have I been out here?" I glanced around, trying to make sense of how I ended up face down in a pile of trash outside my place of work.

"Not too long. When you never came in from tossing the trash I got worried."

Likely. Eric was probably more worried about being named in a potential law suit.

"I'm fine... I think." I struggled to remember what had happened. The only memory I had couldn't be real. It involved a wolf and a strange guy with wings. Evidently I managed to pass out and hit my head on a trash can. Because that's normal.

"Are you sure? Do you think you can walk?"

"Yeah, I can walk." The alternative was to let him carry me inside. Despite his good looks, Eric's personality nullified any desire to have him hold me, even if walking seemed like an insurmountable task at the moment. Out of necessity, I accepted his outstretched hand and leaned heavily on his shoulder. My head continued to throb, and all I wanted to do was get home and lie down.

He put me down on the couch in the break room. The worn sofa wasn't a place I ever wanted to lay my head, considering it was twenty years old and had probably never been cleaned, but I didn't have a choice. The world was spinning.

"Did you hit your head?" Eric asked, taking a seat next to me. His muscular arm blocked my view of the room.

I reached up and touched the knot forming on the back of my head. "Yes. I have no idea how."

"Only you would do something that ridiculous." He routinely made fun of me, but something was off. Then again, I'd hit my head so maybe everything was off.

"Can you get my purse? It's in that locker." I pointed around him to where I'd stowed my stuff.

"Sure." He walked across the room and retrieved my ancient knock-off Gucci. He handed it to me, and I fished out my phone.

"Are you calling someone to get you?" He settled in next to me. The couch sunk down from the extra weight.

"Yeah. My cousin." I hit Rhett's name on my contacts list.

"Casey?" Rhett answered after two rings. Five years older than me, Rhett and I didn't hang out much, but he was being seriously awesome by letting me crash in the spare bedroom (read closet) in his apartment in the Village.

"Any chance you could walk down to Coffee Heaven?"

"Sure…but is there a particular reason why?" He sounded distracted, which probably meant he was buried in his research. A twinge of guilt went through me when I thought about bothering him, but asking Eric to walk me home was out of the question, and we were the only two closing.

"I kind of passed out and hit my head."

"What?" Shuffling, followed by a door slamming, let me know he was on his way. I worked a few blocks from Rhett's place, so I knew it wouldn't be long. "Hold tight. I'll be right there."

"I could have walked you home." Eric stood up, probably getting ready to unlock the front door for Rhett. He opened his mouth like he wanted to say more, but he quickly shut it.

"Rhett doesn't mind."

Eric mumbled something incomprehensible before stomping off through the doorway. I didn't really get him. He was a jerk to me most of the time, but then other times he got almost protective.

Eric returned minutes later with Rhett on his heels.

"You okay, Case?" Rhett kneeled down in front of me. As usual, his brown hair was all rumpled, and it looked like he hadn't showered yet. It was ten o'clock at night.

"I think so."

"What happened to her?" He looked at Eric, an unspoken accusation hanging in the air.

"I'm not positive. She went out to toss the trash and when I came out to look for her, she was on the ground."

"Next time, throw out the trash yourself." Rhett helped me up. "Casey won't be coming in to work tomorrow."

"Hey. I will so. I need the shift." My savings were dwindling, and that didn't bode well for going back to school the next semester.

Rhett shook his head. "No, you don't."

"I do. Eric, don't find someone to cover me. I'll be in."

"See you tomorrow, Bates." Eric blatantly ignored my cousin and called me by my last name. No matter how many times I reminded him that I preferred he use my first name, he disregarded the request.

"Night," I called just before the door closed behind us, leaving us in the brisk night air.

"You're a glutton for punishment, kid."

"Who are you calling kid?" I linked my arm with Rhett's as we walked past Washington Square Park. I was feeling better but was still light headed.

"You're nineteen. You're a kid."

"I don't feel like one." Working full time and trying to support myself on only a step above minimum wage had been an eye opening experience, even with the ridiculously cheap rent I owed Rhett.

"Usually you don't act like one. Rushing to get back to your crap job is acting like a kid."

"It's the only job I have, and I need it." Beggars can't be choosers in New York when it comes to making money with only a high school diploma and almost no previous work experience. Funny how working at a summer camp doesn't do much for a resume.

"Or you could pick a less expensive school and not worry so much about financial aid."

"Says the guy working on his PhD at NYU?"

"Hey, they pay me now." He opened the exterior door to our building.

"They didn't when you were an undergrad."

He let go of me so he could unlock the inner door. You had to tug on the door at the same time you turned the key or it didn't work. The super was supposed to fix the temperamental lock months before. "True, but my scholarship covered most of it."

I stood just inside the entryway. "All right, can't argue with that."

"Can you make it?" He gestured to the stairs. We lived in a third floor walkup.

"Maybe." I headed toward the stairs that currently looked like mountains. "It's worth a try."

Ten minutes later, I was propped up on the couch with a bottle of water. Rhett worried over me for another few minutes before I made him get back to work. I flipped through the channels, hoping for some random movie. There was absolutely nothing on, so I settled for the local news.

Another animal attack has been reported in Bryant Park. Authorities have not released the names of the victims, but once again citizens are urged to use caution when frequenting outdoor areas after dark.

I'd seen two other news reports just like it that week, although both reported attacks in different parts of the city. I thought of the wolf in the alley. It must have just been my overactive imagination messing with me. I needed sleep, and lots of it. I switched off the TV and closed my eyes. I didn't even have the energy to move to my room.

Soar is available now!

Want to stay up to date on Alyssa Rose Ivy's releases? Join her mailing list: http://eepurl.com/ktlSj

23133595R00142

Made in the USA
San Bernardino, CA
06 August 2015